Bonded by Love

The Heart Never Lies

D. Brown-Newton

Chapter One (Chink)

"LJ, your father will be here soon; get these toys up right now," I said, repeating myself for the second time.

I can't believe how hard-headed a two-year-old can be. I've been trying to get him dressed and ready to go. I had been waiting on him to put his toys away for almost an hour now. Lah keeps telling me that I'm too soft when it comes to LJ, and I keep trying to tell him that he's my baby. We were invited to Lah's father's barbeque; he has one every year and invites all of his friends and family. I saw that LJ ignored me again when I looked in his room to see if he was done picking the toys up, and he was nowhere to be found. I decided to just go ahead and put the toys away myself, hearing Lah in the back of my head, telling me that this was the reason why LJ didn't take me seriously. He knows that I'm going to always do it for him.

"Mom, can I have juice?" LJ asked, entering his bedroom.

"No, you can't have any juice. Mommy asked you to put these toys away, and you didn't," I answered.

"Okay, I help," he said.

"LJ, it's okay, I'll help," I said, correcting him.

When LJ and I finished picking up his toys, I gave him a juice box to drink while I packed his bag. By the time I was done getting LJ and myself ready, Lah was walking in the door with Polo, Liem, and baby Paris.

"Hey, babe. I was just going to tell you to come out, but Polo needed to change Paris." Lah greeted me with a kiss.

"Yeah, girl. She spilled juice everywhere. I told somebody not to give it to her," she said, giving Liem the side eye.

"What daddy's baby girl wants, you know she gets," he smiled, kissing Paris' chubby cheeks.

We arrived at Lah's father's house, and I had to say that his house was beautiful. I always knew that his daddy had money, but I didn't know it was this kind of money. The house was a mini-mansion, reminding me of the house from the movie, Diary of a Mad Black Woman. We were escorted to the back of the house where the party was being held. As soon as we reached the backyard, the smell of good barbeque assaulted my nose as my mouth watered. LJ took off running; he had a very bad habit of doing that as soon as you let his hand go.

"I'll go get him," I said to Lah as I followed in the direction he ran off to.

I was just a few steps from where LJ had run off to, and here I was, trying to figure out who in the hell was the fine man talking to my son. I was in awe, just as I was a few seconds ago when I was admiring the house. I walked over to where they were standing and tried to find my voice.

"LJ, how many times do I have to tell you that you can't just run off?" I said to my child.

"He was in good hands; he wanted to get into the pool, and I was just telling him that he needed to put on his swim trunks. So we were just about to come find his parents," the fine gentleman answered.

"Thank you; he just took off. He has a very bad habit of running as soon as you let go of his hand. I'm his mother, Chasity, and you are?" I asked, extending my hand.

"My bad, shorty. My name is Rellz," he replied in his deep, baritone voice.

"Nice to meet you, and thanks again. LJ, let's go and get you changed so that you can get into the pool," I said, taking LJ's hand and walking off.

I walked away, throwing my hips from side to side because I wanted Mr. Rellz to see exactly what I was working with. After being pregnant with LJ, my hips and ass were on fleek. Don't ask me why I wanted him to see what I was working with because the only answer I could possibly come up with would be that his ass was fine. I walked back over to where Lah was standing, talking to his father. I needed to let him know that LJ needed to be changed because he wanted to get into the pool.

"How are you doing, Chasity? I was just telling your husband that I really appreciate you guys coming out," his father smiled.

"You're welcome, and thanks for inviting us," I responded.

"No thanks needed; we're family. You guys go and enjoy yourselves, and don't worry too much about the kids. Trust when I say that they are in good hands. I have adults who are helping monitor the kids so the parents can enjoy themselves without worrying too much," he said.

I went looking for my sis so that I could tell her about the fine man that I just saw; she was sitting and talking to a few of the party goers. I decided to wait to tell her, but I went to join her anyway because Lah was being shown off to all of his family on his father's side. It would have been nice for his father to introduce the wife also, but I wasn't sweating it.

"Hey, sis. Where's Liem?" I asked, not caring that I interrupted the conversation she was having with an older guest.

"I'm guessing he's wherever the food is, and now that I think about it, he never came back with something for me to eat," she laughed.

I took Paris out of her hands so that she could go and make sure that Liem was getting her something to eat. She excused herself and headed off to find Liem. I wasn't hungry just yet because LJ and I had a late breakfast, being we didn't get up until noon. Just as I was putting Paris back into her stroller because she had fallen asleep, the fine stranger appeared. Well correction, he told me his name, so he was no longer a stranger.

"Hey again," he greeted.

"Hey," I smiled, looking around to make sure that I didn't see Lah.

"Which family are you related to?" he asked me.

"I'm related to the Hicks family by marriage," I answered.

"So you're married?" he asked, with a smirk on his face.

"I know you see this big ass ring on my finger, just like I see that nice ass ring on your finger," I said. I noticed it now, but I hadn't seen it when I talked to him near the pool.

"Oh, so you peeped that?" he laughed.

"Yeah, I peeped your game. If you wanted to talk about my status you could have said something like, I see that you're married," I said, smiling.

"Well, I'll go a step further. Are you happily married?" he challenged.

"Yes, I'm happily married," I answered him.

"How long have you been married?" he asked, prying.

"I've been married for a few months. Why?" I asked him.

"So, if you've only been married for a few months, how do you know that you're happy?" he laughed.

"I said I've been married for a few months, but I have been with my husband for over two years," I said, wondering why I was telling this man, who I just met minutes ago, my damn business.

"Sounds cool. Is this your little girl?" he asked.

"Nope, this is my niece. I only have one, and you met him already."

"Well, are you happily married?" I asked him, getting all up in his business like he was just in mine.

"Yes, I'm happily married to my wife of three years," he responded.

"Do you have any children, Mr. Happily Married?" I asked him.

"Yes, I have three children – a daughter with my wife, and a son and daughter from previous relationships. Also, my wife and I are raising her two nieces," he answered.

"Wow, five children. I can barely handle the one I've got. He's a handful."

"Yes, five children all under one roof, and I wouldn't change it for anything in the world," he said, smiling.

I wanted to ask how the arrangement came about, but I didn't want to overstep my boundaries – even though his ass was all up in my business. Shit, five kids under one roof. I would be pulling my hair out everyday.

"So, where is your husband, or did you come alone?" he asked.

"He's around here somewhere with his father," I said. "Are you here with the wife and kids?"

"Nah, she had a prior engagement. I'm here with my pops and my boy, Turk."

I was going to ask him who his father was, but Lah walked up. I thought that he was going to be rude or show some type of jealousy, but it wasn't his style to let another man know that he was bothered by his presence. They got to talking and found out that they were cousins - first cousins at that. Lah's father and Rellz's father were brothers. They also found out that they had a lot in common; they had both just met their dads, so they hit it right off. They got on the subject of poker, and the next thing I knew, Rellz was telling Lah to put his money where his mouth was. The poker game was on and popping, with the other men joining in. The night turned out to be perfect; we all had a good time. Lah and Liem were beasts at poker, but I must say that Rellz and Turk were really good, too. By the end of the game, Rellz and Lah were the big winners and were still bickering about who was a better poker player.

I never saw so much damn money on a table before at someone's house; yes, in Vegas, but not at a backyard party. Their asses were serious when it came to poker. It was time for us to call it a night. Rellz and Lah exchanged numbers and promised to hang out with Rellz inviting him to his club. LJ was sleeping, so Lah had to carry him to the car. My ass was exhausted and couldn't wait to get home. We had to drop Polo and Liem off before heading home, but since they weren't too far from us, it didn't take long. I didn't know what it was about Rellz, but I couldn't stop thinking about his ass. I knew that I had no choice but to stop thinking about his fine ass, especially since he and Lah are family. Once we dropped Polo and Liem off, the car was quiet, and I didn't want to continue my naughty thoughts of Mr. Rellz, so I made small talk with Lah.

"Did you have a good time?" I asked him.

"It was cool," he answered, being short - so not like him.

"How did it feel meeting more of your family?" I tried again.

"It felt like I knew some of them all my life; everyone was cool." he said. "So, what was up with you sitting and talking with Rellz like your husband and son weren't in attendance?" he asked.

"I was just talking to him just like I was talking to all the other guests," I said.

"Don't let those new found hips and ass get you fucked up," he joked, and I let go of the breath I was holding.

I was relieved that he was just joking because he had my ass scared to death that he was going to see right through me and accuse me of trying to get with Rellz. Had he known what direction the conversation was really headed in, he wouldn't have been joking. Once we got in the house, I put LJ to bed, showered, and cuddled with my man, causing Rellz to become a distant memory.

Chapter Two (Rellz)

I just got to my club, Onyx, which was located downtown. My security team was waiting on me to give them their work orders for the night because the setup changed weekly. I had no time for any inside jobs at my expense. I enjoyed managing all of my clubs again with the help of Turk and sometimes Kane, when he was able to help out. He's been coping with the death of Rena and taking care of his son, Kendrick, so his time was limited. Tasha expressed that she didn't like that I was back managing the clubs because of all the females that were in attendance every weekend. She made sure to add that she trusted me, but she didn't trust the trifling females that came to the club to bag their next man. I let her know that I was just trying to run a successful business and that I didn't have time for any of the females that tried to get at me every chance that they got.

After giving my security team their detail for the night, I began my ritual that I completed every weekend before the club opened. It consisted of making sure the bars were stocked, VIP section was on point, bathrooms were cleaned, and I always checked to make sure that each floor of the club was on point. I had a cleanup crew that took care of all of those things, but I always had to do the walk through to make sure that they did their job in its entirety.

I tried to convince Tasha to come to the club so that she could see exactly what I do. Once the club is up and running for the night, I'm in my office, doing paperwork and watching the security cameras. The only time that I'm in the club is if I'm needed by one of my staff or if a situation needs to be handled. Turk was coming through tonight to chill, so I'll probably have a few drinks and kick it with him, but that's about it. I was at my desk, going over the inventory report, when someone knocked at my door.

"It's open; come in," I said. I continued to look over the report in front of me because I knew that it was Turk entering my office.

"Yo, my nigga. What's good?" he asked, taking a seat across from me.

"Ain't shit, just going over some paperwork. What's good with you?"

"I'm ready to get my drink on and bag one of these bitches to take home tonight," he said.

"I feel you. Let me finish up here, and we can head down to the bar," I told him.

It was a little after midnight when we decided to head down to the club. Turk's ass wasn't even downstairs for a few seconds before he started flirting with the females. I walked my ass to the bar before he got me caught up in some shit and had Tasha murdering my ass.

"Hey, boss man. What can I get you?" my bartender, Trish, asked me.

"Let me get a Hennessey straight," I told her, as I listened to what was being said into my earpiece.

It was security letting me know that Lah and Liem were at the front. I told them to let those niggas straight up to VIP and to let them know I would be up in a minute. I invited Lah to come and hang out the other night when we were at the family gathering, but I didn't think he would actually take me up on my offer. Like myself, he seemed like the type that didn't trust motherfuckers so easily - family or not. I walked up the stairs to the VIP, passing Turk as he stood against the wall, all up close and personal with some chick. I knew that Turk was one of the reasons Tasha didn't trust my ass at the club. She knew Turk flocked to women, and she figured that I was doing the same shit he was, but I wasn't.

"Hey, cuz. Thanks for coming through," I said, as I walked up on him and Liem, giving them both dap.

"Thanks for the invite, man. I'm loving the vibe, and the music is on point," he said.

"Yeah, the vibe is cool. I have to say that Onyx is my fast paced club; my club, Linx, in midtown, is more of a laid back club for a much older crowd. My DJ, Spinx, always brings out a younger atmosphere at Onyx because he keeps this shit jumping."

"Cool, now I have a place to come to just chill and get my drink on after a stressful week at work," he responded.

"Well, you and your bro are family, so VIP treatment every time you come through this motherfucker," I told him.

"That's love, cuz," he smiled.

"Nothing but love for my fam," I said.

We chilled, talking shit and getting our drink on when Turk finally decided to join us, inviting the chick he was chilling with earlier and a few of her friends. As innocent as it was, I kind of felt guilty after telling Tasha that I would be in my office, handling paperwork. I decided to just have a good time and enjoy the company. The DJ was now playing Jeremih's joint, "Don't Tell Em," and it seemed like all the females hit the dance floor. I watched as the chick that was chilling with Turk stood up, swaying her hips and dancing in front of him. She was giving him a private dance, and he was lying back against the booth, taking her all in. Her girls got up and followed suit; they were dancing provocatively, and it caused my dick to jump, and that was a no no. I signaled for the waitress to get us a couple of more bottles for my guests and me. Just as I finished with the waitress, I looked up and saw Tasha and her home girl, Jasmine, walking over to the booth we were chilling in. I looked up at her to get a feel on her demeanor, and she didn't have a pleasant look on her face. It pissed me off, and I was upset, not with her but with the security detail, because no one gave me a heads up that my wife was in the building and on her way up to VIP.

'Someone fucked up and lost their job tonight,' I thought as I watched her walk over to me. I got up to give her a hug and could feel that she didn't want to return the love. Her hug was forced, and I could tell she was upset.

"Can I speak to you for a second?" she asked. I could feel the attitude seeping off of her ass, and all I could think was, *'Here we go with the bullshit.'*

I let Lah know that I would be right back; I didn't even get the chance to introduce her to my cousin because of the little attitude that she was having. We went to my office, and as soon as we got inside, she started in on me.

"So what happened to you being in your office doing paperwork tonight?" she asked.

"Tash, remember I told you that I met my cousin for the first time at my uncle's crib? Well, I extended an invitation to my club, and he and his bro came through, so Turk and I were just chilling with them, showing them a good time," I said, really not feeling the need to explain myself.

"So showing them a good time includes having bitches chilling and shit?" she asked.

"Tash, did you see me chilling with any females?" I asked her.

"No, I just saw that you were so busy looking at those bitches shaking their asses that you didn't even see me walk up."

"Tash, I saw you way before you walked over; stop with the bullshit. I told you that I'm not on that shit. I'm happily married," I said, grabbing her around her waist and kissing her on her neck.

"Rellz, don't have me fuck you up in your own club." Tasha pushed me off of her.

"How many times do I have to tell you that I only have eyes for your ass?" I said, pulling her back into me and kissing her on the lips.

She didn't pull back this time. She kissed me back, slipping me the tongue and teasing me, and as soon as I got into the kiss, she pulled away.

"What are you doing here anyway? When I was at the crib you didn't mention that you were coming to the club tonight."

"If I would have told you that I was coming through, I wouldn't have caught you chilling with those bitches."

"You would have caught me doing the same thing I was doing, which was nothing. I told you that I'm happily married to your fine ass. Those females don't hold a candle to what I have at home," I whispered in her ear, being honest.

"And you better not forget it," she said, rolling her eyes.

We walked back to the VIP area because she remembered that she just up and left her friend, Jasmine, there. When we got back to the table, everyone was getting along and having a good time. Her friend, Jasmine, was having a conversation with Lah, and he was all smiles and shit. Whatever she was whispering in his ear, he must have been feeling it. I watched as he put his hand between her legs; his ass sure wasn't acting as if he was married.

I broke up the little moment they were having to introduce Tasha to him and his brother, Liem. After the introductions were out of the way, we all continued to get our drink on and enjoy the rest of the night.

Chapter Three (Tasha)

I decided to go to club Onyx and check up on Rellz's ass, so I called and invited my girl, Jasmine, to go out with me. She wasn't really into the club scene, but I assured her that Rellz's club wasn't like the typical club that she was thinking of. When we arrived, I saw his bouncer, Rob, reach for his radio to announce me, but I told him that it wasn't necessary. I informed him that I had just spoken to Rellz, and he knew that I was at the club, and he told me to come to his office. I lied with a straight face, and he fell for it.

I didn't go to his office because Rob let me know that he was no longer in his office. He said that Rellz was now upstairs, chilling in VIP. As soon as I walked up the stairs, I spotted him and saw these thirsty ass bitches shaking their asses at his table, and instantly, I caught an attitude. Jasmine looked at me, knowing I was about to go off. She tried to tell me to chill, talking about the bitches were only dancing, but I wasn't trying to hear her ass. I walked over to him, not even speaking to Turk's ass because like always, he was in some bitch's face. I told Rellz that I needed to speak to his ass because I wanted to know what happened to him having to do paperwork.

Long story short, he told me that his cousin, who he just met for the first time the other night, was at the club, so he was just showing him and his brother a good time. I let the shit slide and decided to just enjoy myself. Jasmine left the club before me because she said she had to get up early in the morning. I knew that her ass was leaving to hook up with Lah's ass because tomorrow was Sunday, so she had to get up early to do what? She doesn't go to church, and her daughter wouldn't be home until later that evening. I told her that it was cool, and she didn't have to drop me off because I decided to wait on Rellz. After Rellz finished what he needed to do at the club, we headed to Ihop to get some breakfast, leaving his head of security to lock up. It seemed as if everyone from the club ended up going to get some breakfast, but we didn't have to wait because Rellz seemed to have groupies, so we were seated right away. I was happy that we got seated right away, but I was starting to feel some type of way because all these fucking bitches knew his ass, which tells me that he must be a regular at the restaurant.

Our server, Sophie, was getting on my last nerve. She kept being touchy feely with Rellz, and I was two seconds away from bashing that bitch in the head with the coffee pitcher. Rellz's ass was smiling in this bitch's face like I wasn't sitting across the table from his ass, so I made it my business to kick his ass under the table, letting him know not to fucking play with me.

"What was that for?" he asked, smiling like the shit was funny.

"You've got one more time to smile up in this bitch's face. Keep playing with me, and I'm going to show you and that bitch that I'm not to be fucked with," I whispered to his ass, meaning every fucking word.

I knew that my man was fine and that women were going to flirt with him, but I'd be damned if a bitch was going to do it in my face. He can act like the shit is nothing, but I'm not having it on my watch. When the bitch, Sophie, came back and touched him on his arm as she spoke to him, that was the last straw.

"Excuse me. It's Sophie, right?"

"Yes, what can I do for you?" she asked.

"What you can do for me is keep all that flirting that you're doing to yourself, and if your hands touch another part of my man's body, we're going to have a fucking problem," I told the bitch, not caring that I was not whispering anymore, but I was being kind of loud.

"I'm sorry if you took my being courteous as flirting. I do apologize," she said, trying to play me like I was a dumb bitch.

"So what part of being courteous includes you ignoring me and continuing to flirt with my man like I'm not sitting here?" I asked her ass.

"Like I said, ma'am, I wasn't flirting, and I already apologized if I made you feel like I was flirting with your man. Again, I apologize," she said, speaking like she had an attitude now.

"No problem; just don't let the shit happen again," I said with much attitude, letting her know that her attitude didn't faze me one bit.

When she walked off, Rellz looked at me and shook his head like he thought I was going to keep letting that shit slide. His ass knows how I give it up, so he should have stopped the bitch when she did it the first time.

I didn't even want to eat the food that she brought out. I left that shit sitting in the same spot where she placed it. Rellz didn't have a problem eating his breakfast, and he dug in like he didn't have a care in the world, but I did.

"So you're not going to eat?" he asked me with his mouth full of pancakes.

"Hell no. For all I know that bitch spit in my fucking food."

"Tash, that girl didn't do anything to your food. You need to stop the bullshit and eat your breakfast," he said, laughing.

"No, thank you. When I get home, I'll make me something to eat," I said, rolling my eyes at his ass.

"I don't know what I'm going to do with your ass," he said, stuffing a piece of bacon in his mouth.

"If these thirsty bitches learned some fucking respect, you wouldn't have a problem trying to figure out what to do with me. If I saw a good looking man, yes, I'm going to look, but you better believe I'm not going to do no fucking thirsty flirting and disrespecting that man's girl in the process."

"Well Tash, you don't have to let these bitches know that you're bothered by the shit because trust, that shit doesn't faze me."

"Well, I can't tell because your ass was smiling with the bitch from the time she walked her stink ass to the fucking table. And why is it that we were able to skip all of the people that were waiting anyway?"

"Because I'm the fucking man," he said, smiling like I was fucking playing with him.

When he finished his meal, he left a tip on the table, and I picked that shit up, deciding to be petty. Fuck that bitch.

Chapter Four (Lah)

"Yeah, suck this dick," I said, between moans, as I grabbed the back of her head, pumping in and out of her mouth.

I had no intentions of following Jasmine back to her crib, but when she was whispering in my ear all of the things she was going to do to my dick, I was game. This bitch's head game was on point; I never came this damn fast from getting no head. I asked her ass if she had any condoms because I was ready to hit, and as much as I wanted to hit, if she didn't have any condoms, this session was definitely over. I refuse to run up in any bitch, other than my wife, raw. She unwrapped the condom and put it on with her mouth. This bitch had skills. I bent her ass over the sofa and fucked the shit out of her. I'm not going to lie; this bitch's pussy was on point, causing me to slow down because I wanted to savor the moment for as long as possible.

We fucked for hours; she was a straight freak, and by the time I woke up, it was after two in the afternoon. I have never stayed out all night, and I knew that I fucked up. I reached for my phone in my pants pocket and noticed that I had like ten missed calls from Chink. I decided not to call her or return any of her text messages. I was just going to hop in the shower and get my ass home. When I got home, Chink was sitting in the living room, reading on her Kindle. I walked over to greet her with a kiss that she refused. Her body language also let me know that she had an attitude, and she wasn't going to try and hear shit that I was about to spit to her.

"Where the fuck were you last night that you couldn't answer your phone or pick up your phone to call your fucking wife to let me know that you were okay?" she asked, putting her Kindle down on the table and looking like she was ready to fuck me up.

"Babe, I hung out with Rellz at his club. I had too much to drink, so I crashed at his place last night," I lied.

"So how is it that you didn't leave the club with Liem, your brother? You do remember your brother, right? I doubt if he would have left you at a club by yourself, with you being intoxicated to the point to where you couldn't pick up your phone or drive home," she stated.

"Liem didn't stay at the club long; when he left, I hadn't even started drinking," I said, not knowing what else to say.

"I've known you for how long? And not one time have you ever gotten intoxicated to the point to where you couldn't drive or be on point with your surroundings, so Lah, miss me with the bullshit."

"Babe, he had us chilling in VIP, and we were popping bottles all night, just having a good time, and I had too much to drink. My bad."

"You know what, Lah? I know that you're selling me bullshit right now, and only because I don't have any proof, I'm going to let it slide. Since your ass couldn't find your way home last night, make sure you don't find your way to my bed tonight, and crash your ass on this couch." Chink stood up, grabbed her tablet, and walked upstairs.

I didn't bother to follow her up the stairs because she was right, and I deserved to sleep on the couch tonight. I went into the kitchen to get something to eat and couldn't help but think about the sex session that Jasmine put on my ass. My dick was hard as shit just thinking about all the freaky shit she did to me. I have never had a bitch suck both of my balls and jerk my dick at the same time, until I bust in her mouth. Her ass swallowed every fucking drop without gagging or running to the bathroom to throw up, letting me know that all of the others were amateurs. Chink's ass used to be on point, but since she had LJ, I only got special treatment on special occasions, so you know what that means. My dick only gets to feel the warmth of her mouth like twice a year. I hate to say it, but I'm definitely going to be hitting Jasmine's ass off again.

Chapter Five (Jasmine)

I was pissed at Tasha at first for dragging me to the club to chase after Rellz's cheating ass, but after seeing Lah, all was forgiven. His ass was fine, and I definitely wanted to take his ass home. I didn't care that he had a ring on his finger either because what I want, I get, and his ass would be no different. Just as I was about to reminisce about my night with his fine ass, someone knocked at the door. I wasn't expecting anyone, so I had no idea who would be knocking on my door on a Sunday.

"Rellz, what are you doing here?" I asked him, letting him in.

"So now I need an invitation to see you? Don't be acting all brand new. Did you fuck him?" he asked me.

"Excuse you? Just in case you forgot, my name is Jasmine and not Tasha. Who I fuck is my business," I told his ass.

"Don't fucking play with me, Jas. I introduced that nigga to you as my cousin, and you still fucked him. So you're going to fuck us both?"

"Rellz, I'm single, so again, who I choose to fuck is my business and of no concern to you."

"Keep talking that fly shit, and I'm going to put something in your fucking mouth to shut that ass up," he said, grabbing his dick.

"As long as it's long, thick, and juicy, shut me the hell up." I got down on my knees in front of him, taking him into my mouth.

Bet his ass wasn't thinking about the next man anymore as I deep throated his ass. I had him moaning like a little bitch. He was assaulting my mouth, hitting the back of my throat, but all that shit did was turn me on. I put pressure on his dick, with my lips, until I had him releasing all of his babies down my throat. I sat on his face and rode his tongue as he dipped it in and out of my wet pussy. I let him fuck me in my ass, and I used my right hand to play in my pussy, rubbing it in a circular motion as I squeezed my left nipple with my left hand. My orgasm was explosive as the sensation from all three of my sensitive spots sent a pleasurable bolt throughout my body.

I laid back on the couch and put my legs around his neck. He lifted my ass off the couch, until it was hanging off the edge, and he held onto my hips, entering me roughly. He was being a beast, and I knew why, but there was no need for him to make me say that this was his pussy because this pussy belonged to whoever was fucking it at the time. His ass must have forgot who he was fucking because I fucked with the best of them, and his ass was no different. I tightened my pussy muscles on his dick and fucked him like the bad bitch that I was. I had that ass screaming like a bitch in two and a half seconds as I pulled all of the remaining cum up out of his ass.

I know that some might say that I'm grimy for fucking with my friend's man and even grimier for fucking his cousin less than twenty-four hours ago, but guess what? I don't give a fuck. I do me, how I see fit. That's how it has always been, and that's how it is always going to be. No, I'm not a hoe; I just realized that niggas will never be loyal, so I learned to play them, just like they play women. The only difference is that I'm not cheating on a significant other. Growing up, I've been used by so-called friends and lovers. They claimed to have love for me only to use and abuse me, so I made a vow to myself to always live my life as I see fit and to never give my heart to anyone ever again. Fuck friends and fuck love is how I'm giving it up.

Yes, Tasha has been a good friend, but that's how it always starts out before they start showing their true colors. It's easy for me to say that she's my friend, but it really has no meaning to me because they are just words. As far as me feeling bad about fucking with her husband, I didn't because

I feel that I did her a favor. I told her that his ass was nothing but a cheating dog, and I was right. He knew that he was married, but that didn't stop him from begging me to eat the pussy. He was just like all of these other thirsty ass nigga who didn't give a fuck that they had a girl or wife at home. They all throw it away for a cute face and a fat ass.

Trust when I say that I didn't want to become this person, but when you give your all to a person and treat them with love and respect, they give you their ass to kiss and fuck you over all the time. When I met my ex-boyfriend, Que, he was my first love, and I loved him more than I loved myself, believing that he felt the same way about me. Boy, was I wrong, and if I had never gotten that call from my mother all those years ago, I probably would still be in that twisted relationship.

I remembered the day so clearly. I told Que that my grandmother had passed away, and I was leaving the next day with my mother to go to Virginia. He said that he wasn't able to go with me because of his job, and I understood. It was on short notice, and she wasn't any kin to him, so his job would have had a problem giving him the time off. I was supposed to be gone for a week, but I left to go home the day after the funeral, leaving my mom to get my grandmother's affairs in order. When I got to my apartment, Que's car was in the parking lot, and I felt better already because just seeing my man always made me feel better. I needed him right now because my grandmother's death really hit me hard.

I walked inside my small, one-bedroom apartment, leaving my luggage near the door. I expected him to be sitting in front of the television, playing the game, but he wasn't there. As I neared the bedroom that we shared, I heard the soft music playing, but it still didn't register. I figured that he was watching television, and the music was coming from whatever he was watching. Nothing could have prepared me for what I saw behind my bedroom door. My best friend, Tony, had Que bent over the bed, fucking him in the same position that Que fucked me in whenever we had sex. They made my favorite position look so dirty. I felt sick to my stomach as I ran from the bedroom, to the bathroom down the hall, throwing up everything that I had consumed that morning.

Que couldn't even look at me when I came out of the bathroom, and the only words that my best friend of eight years, Tony, had to say to me was, "Girl, I told you his ass wasn't shit." I had been physically and mentally fucked up since that day, and that's the reason I felt the way I did about friends and love. Que always had a thuggish swag about him;

shit, that's what attracted me to him, and I would have never thought that he was on the down low.

I cut all ties in Atlanta because I was hurt and embarrassed, so I was on the next thing smoking and have been in New York for four years, never looking back. It was also rumored that my family knew that Que was messing around with Tony, so I kind of felt betrayed, and all I had was me, myself, and I. My mother never sold my grandmother's house in Virginia. She decided to stay, and she wanted me to come there with her, but I declined, cutting ties with her as well. I didn't even realize that I was crying. I wiped my tears away quickly because none of them deserved my tears. After Rellz left, I did a little cleaning because my daughter, Ariel, would be home from her babysitter's house in a few hours. Once I had my place in order, I grabbed a glass of wine and called up Tasha to see what she was up to on this Sunday evening.

Chapter Six (Polo)

I was trying hard not to go off on Liem's ass because I wasn't feeling his ass lying for his brother. I understand that Lah was his brother, but lying to me will get his ass cut. We just dropped Paris off to my mother's house because, once again, Lah's newfound family was having a get together. This time the get together was going to be at his cousin, Rellz's, house, so we would get to meet his wife and a few family members that weren't at the barbeque we attended at Lah's father house. Chink was still mad with Lah, so I just hoped that they would come out and have a good time without arguing.

We arrived at Rellz's house, and I must say, it was just as beautiful as Lah's father place. I couldn't wait for the day that I could live in a big house like this one. It had an oversized, three car garage. I could see that he had a swimming pool, basketball court, and much more, but that's all I could see from where I was standing. I was highly impressed when I saw that he had valet parking. Liem told me to stop acting like a groupie, but I didn't care; I felt like I was at the house of someone famous. The inside of the house was just as impressive, and yes, when Rellz's wife offered Liem and me a tour of the house, I gladly accepted.

The house had expensive hardwood floors in all of the bedrooms, the kitchen had granite counters, hardwood cabinets, high-end appliances, and even the floor was marble and granite. I loved every inch of the house, but the best part of the house was the master bedroom that was spacious with an exquisite view from the balcony. Tasha and Lah had arrived by the time our tour was over. They seemed to have made up because she was in a good mood. I went and greeted them both, even though I wanted to punch Lah in the throat.

"Hey, sis. How long have you been here?" I asked her.

"We just got here. How long have you been here?" she questioned.

"We've been here for a good twenty minutes. Rellz's wife gave Liem and me a tour of the house, and I absolutely love it."

"Shit, all I saw was the outside and the room we are sitting in, and I love what I've seen so far. I can imagine what the rest of the house looks like," she laughed, looking around.

"Well, I'm sure that Rellz's wife, Tasha, will give you a tour of the house if you and Lah want to see it."

"Maybe later. Let's go see where Lah and Liem ran off too," she said, taking my hand and pulling me with her.

"Knowing Liem, his ass is probably where the food is, just like the last get together. His ass couldn't stop talking about all of the food on our way home that night," I laughed, causing her to laugh too.

When we walked into the dining area, just as I thought, Liem was fixing him a plate and acting like he didn't just eat less than an hour ago. Lah was over in the corner of the room, talking to some female like he wasn't here with his wife. I looked at Chink, and she looked at me, and it was on as we walked over, breaking up their little conversation.

"Hey, Lah. Who's your little friend?" I asked him.

"I'm Jasmine, and you are?" she asked, with a fake smile on her face.

"I'm Polo, and this is his wife, Chink," I replied, rolling my eyes at the bitch.

"How do you know my husband?" Chink asked.

"I met him at the club the other night, and we hit it off. He's cool people." She spoke with a smirk on her face.

I saw Chink's facial expression change, and I was waiting for Lah to intervene before the shit got out of hand, but his ass just stood there, looking stupid. I was ready to pop off on both of their asses. I didn't know why the cat had Lah's tongue, but he better find that shit, sooner than later, because although I didn't want to disrespect Rellz's home, I had no problem doing so. I decided to put a stop to the stare down that Jasmine and Chink were having because I was getting more pissed off by the minute.

"Well, it was nice meeting you, Jasmine. See you around," I said, praying that she took that as her queue to keep it moving.

"Lah, I'm going to go mix and mingle. I'll get up with you later." Jasmine spoke to Lah, but she was looking at Chink, and it took everything in me not to slap her ass.

"You and that bitch seemed too familiar with each other to have just met the other night. Is she the reason you didn't bring your ass home the night you supposedly crashed at Rellz's crib?" Chink questioned him.

"Chink, I just met her at the club the other night, like she said. She's best friends with Rellz's wife, Tasha," he whispered.

"So when you crashed here the other night, did she crash here too?" she asked him.

"No, she didn't. Now stop bugging for no reason. Let's go and have a good time and not spoil it on some bullshit," he said.

"Do you want something to eat?" he asked her once he saw Liem come back with a plate for me and him.

"No, I don't want anything to eat, but you go ahead," she told him, walking off.

"Polo, his ass said that he crashed here the night that they went to the club, but his ass wasn't familiar with anything in this house. He was acting like he was just seeing it for the first time," she whispered to me once I made it over to her.

"Chink, he did say that he was intoxicated, so it could be that he doesn't remember," I said, even though I didn't believe it myself.

"Yeah, but he remembered that trick that he was just talking to. My gut is telling me that they did more than just meet," she said, giving Liem the side eye, but he continued to eat like he wasn't listening to our conversation.

I told her to just let it go for now and try to enjoy herself because getting stressed out wasn't going to help the situation. Inside I was pissed off as I watched the bitch, Jasmine, watching Lah's every move from the corner she was sitting in. She wasn't even trying to be discreet about the bullshit. I even watched as Lah made eye contact and smiled at the bitch. I wasn't going to say anything to Chink right now because it could be just a little innocent flirting, but my blood was boiling.

Tasha came and sat with me and Chink. She introduced herself to Chink because she hadn't met her yet. We sat and talked among ourselves once the guys started up a poker game. She was really cool, and I didn't know how she got hooked up with her friend, Jasmine, because she was a snake. Instead of her being over here, chilling with the females, her ass was at the table, playing poker with the men. I didn't trust that bitch as far as I could throw her ass, and Tasha better watch that bitch because she's not to be trusted. One thing I will say about Liem was that he's very respectful around me. He's not going to disrespect me by flirting with another female, knowing that I'm in attendance, and he's not going to let a female disrespect me either. Just watching how the rest of the men were hanging on to this bitch's every word, and smiling and enjoying her flirting, was pissing me off.

I knew that Chink was trying really hard to stay in her seat, and I just knew that it would only be a matter of seconds before she would continue to watch the scene before her without saying anything. Lah knew how she was, so for him to allow the bitch to continue being all up in his face tells me that he either fucked the bitch or he was planning on fucking the bitch. Tasha asked Chink a question, but she didn't even hear her because she was now watching Jasmine dancing like a fucking slut in front of the men. Out of all the songs that played, this bitch decided to jump up and dance to "Like Me" by Jeremih, changing the words from fuck with a nigga like me to with a bitch like me. She made the mistake of mimicking a lap dance in front of Lah, and Chink jumped up quickly, without warning. She grabbed Jasmine by her hair and tossed the bitch. Nobody intervened because we were all shell-shocked for a minute because, like I said, there was no warning. She didn't say any words; she just grabbed the bitch.

"What the fuck is your problem?" she asked, getting up off the floor.

"Bitch, if you ever dance up on my fucking man like that again, I will break your fucking face," Chink said, poking her in the forehead with every word.

"Chink, chill," Lah said, trying to pull her away, but she pulled away from him.

"Why do you have this trick dancing all up in your face like you're single?" she asked, now in his face.

"Why are you acting all insecure? All I was doing was dancing. You're acting like I was trying to fuck him," Jasmine stated.

"Bitch, I don't have an insecure bone in my body, but I do have a problem when a trick doesn't have enough respect not to shake her ass in a married man's face," Chink said to her.

"Jasmine, she's right. That shit was wrong, and you need to apologize," Tasha chimed in.

"Tasha, are you serious? All I was doing was dancing. I'm not about to apologize for something that I didn't do."

"Come on now. You had your ass in his face, so that was disrespectful knowing that he's married, and his wife is here. And don't get me wrong, it's not all your fault because he should have checked your ass so that his wife didn't have to. All I ask is that everyone stops disrespecting my home. We are all adults here, so it shouldn't be a problem with everyone being respectful to each other," Tasha said, trying to be the voice of reason.

"I'm sorry if you feel that I disrespected you by dancing too close to your husband, and Tasha, I apologize to you as well. I didn't mean to start any drama. You know that I'm flirtatious, but I meant no harm. Again, I apologize," she said, walking off.

Chapter Seven (Chink)

I'm bugging right now because I don't know what happened with Lah overnight, but he has never been this fucking disrespectful. How the fuck was he going to have this bitch dancing up on him like that with me sitting in the same fucking room and not tell that bitch to fall back? I swear I tried to be respectful of Tasha and Rellz's house, but her friend was pushing it. To think that I came here telling myself to keep my distance from Rellz, which I was doing a good job of by the way, to have this motherfucker come up in here, acting like he's fucking single. My gut is telling me that he fucked this bitch already, and I put my son's life on it. This nigga wants to play fucking games; I can play them too, and he better believe that I will be the better player. I stood out on the balcony for almost twenty minutes, trying to calm myself down, and this nigga has yet to come and apologize and to make sure I was okay. That further tells me that he fucked this bitch, and she has already got his fucking nose open. I heard someone walk out onto the balcony, and I was hoping it was Lah, but it wasn't. It was Rellz.

"Are you okay?" he asked me.

Damn, why couldn't his ass stay where the fuck he was? I was doing a good job of avoiding his ass. Now he was standing a few inches away from me, looking good. His ass was in simple attire, nothing special, but his body was still on display as I briefly imagined his muscular arms wrapped around me.

"Hello?" he said, bringing me back to the question at hand.

"I'm fine. Thanks for asking." I blushed.

"No problem. I didn't see you come back, so I just came to check up on you to make sure you were good."

"Yes, I'm good. I'm going to have a drink and try to enjoy myself."

"Yeah, you do that because I don't like this look on you," he said, smiling.

"Thanks, but like I said, I'm good now, and again, thanks for checking on me." I smiled.

"Okay, if you're good, I'm good. Now I can go back and kick some ass in poker," he said, walking out.

That shit just pissed me off all over again. Another man came and checked on me, and Lah didn't make his way to check on me yet. I wiped at my tears because I refused to let that bitch, or Lah's ass, see that I was still bothered by the shit. I tell you one thing, if either of them get out of pocket again, Lah is going to see a side of me that he has yet to meet. When I got back downstairs, the bitch was still at the poker table, and his ass was still sitting there like a lovesick puppy. He was the one talking about he couldn't live without me, he loved me, and he wasn't thinking about anybody else. Bullshit.

"You good, sis?" Polo asked me.

"Yeah, I'm good. I don't even know why I let that shit faze me."

"It has nothing to do with fazing you. You did the right thing and let that bitch know that she won't be disrespecting you like you're not here. Had it been anywhere else, that bitch would have been done, and you know that."

"Yeah, I know how you give it up, sis. Thanks for always having my back," I said, hugging her.

"Always." She hugged me back.

The rest of the night was without incident. Lah's ass finally came and apologized and made sure that the rest of the night was spent with me. Rellz had the music blasting, and everyone was dancing and having a good time. I saw that the trick was being flirtatious with Rellz too, so maybe she did just like to flirt with the opposite sex, but she needs to not flirt with men that belong to someone else because that's the quickest way to get the bitch killed.

I excused myself to call my aunt. I wanted to make sure that LJ went down without giving her any problems. She said that he was down for the count, so I went back to enjoying myself. Tasha was mad cool, and we agreed to hook up and have a girl's night minus her friend, Jasmine, because I wasn't interested in hanging anywhere with that bitch. We said our goodbyes and headed home. I had a good time, but my ass was tired and a little intoxicated. Once in the car, the bullshit that happened earlier started to eat at me, and because I'm not one to bite my tongue, I asked Lah what I had been wanting to ask him all night.

"Did you sleep with her?" I asked, causing him to swerve the car.

"Hell no. I didn't sleep with anybody. What the fuck are you talking about now?"

"Nigga, don't act like you're fucking slow. You know exactly who, and what, the fuck I'm talking about."

"Chink, how many times do I have to tell you that I'm not interested in anyone but you?" he asked with a stupid look on his face. This nigga was lying.

"So why the fuck did that bitch feel comfortable enough to have her ass all up in your face, knowing you weren't going to check her ass?"

"I didn't check her ass because all she was doing was dancing. I'm going to need your ass to stop acting so fucking insecure. It's not a good look on you," he had the nerve to say.

"Oh really? So I'm acting insecure because I don't want a bitch with her ass in your face being disrespectful, knowing that I was sitting right there? So tell me how does it make you feel to know that your cousin, Rellz, came to check on me when my own husband didn't come to do it?" I said, once again being petty and not giving a fuck.

"What the fuck do you mean that nigga came to check on you?" he barked.

"Just what the fuck I said. He came upstairs to make sure that I was okay when my sorry excuse of a fucking husband didn't feel the need to."

"Chink, don't get fucked up. Keep thinking I'm the one to fuck with if you want. If that nigga felt the need to come and check on you, then he had to feel comfortable to know that it would be okay to do so. So tell me what the fuck you and that nigga got going on," he said, trying to flip the same shit that I just said to him on me. Typical.

"Ha, you're funny, and just for the record, you're not fucking shit up over here, and remember, I wasn't the one who had a nigga all up on me, with his dick all in my face. In case you forgot, that was your bitch ass violating." I was getting pissed off at his ass now and wishing I hadn't even said anything because he gave me a fucking headache.

"Yeah, okay. I can show you better than I can tell you. Let me catch you in any nigga's face, and see what happens," he said, turning the radio on, letting me know the conversation was over.

"Now watch me whip, now watch me nae nae, now watch me whip whip, now watch me nae nae," I sung, pissing him off.

When we got home, I went straight upstairs, stripped out of my clothes, and hopped in the shower. When I was done, I made sure to put on some granny panties - the ones I wear when it's that time of the month. I also made sure to put on a cotton nightgown that went down below my knees because I wanted to send a clear message to his ass to not even think about touching me tonight. When he came into the room and saw what I was wearing, he instantly caught an attitude, grabbing his pillow and the blanket off the bed, and leaving out of the room. I hope he didn't think I was upset because he was already in the doghouse and sleeping on the couch anyway. I went out to the linen closet, grabbed me another blanket, and took my ass to sleep.

Chapter Eight (Liem)

"What's wrong with you?" I asked Polo because she had been walking around like she had an attitude and not talking to me since we left Rellz's house.

"You already know what's wrong with me. I don't appreciate how your fucking brother tried to play my sis tonight," she said.

"Polo, what does that have to do with us? His relationship is just that - his relationship," I replied.

"See that's the shit I'm talking about. Right is right, and wrong is wrong. His ass sat there and let that skanky bitch dance with her ass all up in his face, knowing that Chink was sitting right there. He was wrong for that shit, and you know it."

"You're right; he was wrong for that shit, but like I said, that has nothing to do with us. Chink handled it, so why am I getting backlash behind my brother's shit. I didn't have no bitch with her ass in my face."

"Because if Lah is out there fucking around, you know about it and are condoning the bullshit because you're doing the same fucking shit," she accused.

"Babe, why does this have to be our fight? I didn't do shit, and if Lah is doing anything, I don't know anything about it, but I'm not going to lie. Even if I did, it's not my business."

"Is it not your business because when you were out there, fucking around, he made it his business not to say anything?" she continued, and I was getting pissed because we had gotten past that. Why was she bringing the shit back up?

"Polo, yes, we went through what we went through, but I promise you that I haven't been with, or tried to be with, anyone. So again, let's not make what Lah did tonight about us. We're in a good place, and that's where I want to stay."

"That's where I want to stay too, but I'm not going to tolerate you lying to me for your brother. If I find out that you lied to me, then we are going to be right back at the same place we were," she responded.

"I promise you that Lah didn't tell me anything about him and that girl, Jasmine, or any other female," I said, being honest.

"Yeah, if you're telling the truth, you have nothing to worry about," she added, walking off.

I went and sat on the couch. I pulled my phone out to send Lah a text because I was a little pissed at his ass for allowing that bullshit to go down like that tonight. Yes, we all do our dirt, but there's a respect factor in that shit, and he played himself tonight for even allowing that bullshit to go down like that. I don't know what the fuck had gotten into his ass because the Lah I knew would have never let that shit go down like that. I was just as shocked as Polo that he had disrespected his wife like that, but I couldn't say that shit to him at the time. I went upstairs an hour later to see if she had cooled off and was ready to start acting like my wife again, but she was already sleeping. I took my disappointed ass to shower, got in bed, cuddled up next to her, and went to sleep. I woke up to the smell of Polo cooking breakfast. I washed my face and brushed my teeth before going downstairs.

"I thought you were mad at me?" I asked her.

"I just wanted to apologize for last night. I shouldn't have taken out the anger that I felt towards Lah on you," she said, kissing me on my lips.

"Babe, you have to know how to separate your friendship with Chink and our relationship. I understand how you felt about the situation, and like I said, Lah was dead wrong, but you can't blame me for his actions or go to bat for Chink when it comes to her relationship. At the end of the day, that's her husband, and it's her who has to deal with him, not you. You can be there to listen, and even give advice, but what you did last night was unfair to me," I declared.

"I know that now, and it will never happen again. I promise."

We sat down and had breakfast together before going to pick Paris up from her mother's house. We stayed over at her mom's house for a little while before heading home. Once at home, I didn't go inside because last night, I had spoken to Lah and told him that I wanted to meet up for a drink and talk to him about something, so that's where I was headed. I know that I told Polo that it was none of our business, but I know when my brother is acting out of character, and I wanted to see what was up with his ass. I pulled up to SoHo Bar, where we agreed to meet, and went inside to see if he had arrived, and he had.

"Hey, bro. What's going on?" he asked me as I sat at the table he was sitting at.

I watched him as he was all into his phone, smiling and shit as he went back and forth, texting whoever was texting him. I wanted to snatch the phone out of his hand, but I didn't. I waited patiently for him to acknowledge me. Yes, he greeted me, but he was acting like I wasn't sitting here.

"What did you need to speak to me about?" he asked, finally putting his phone down and giving me his attention.

"Bro, I'm just trying to figure out what the hell is going on with you."

"What do you mean, what's going on with me? I'm good." He picked his phone up and answered yet another text message.

"Bro, that shit the other night was way out of your character. Why did you allow that bitch to disrespect your wife like that? The Lah that I know would have checked that bitch for doing some dumb shit like that."

"Bro, the bitch was just dancing, and I just feel that Chink and Polo didn't have to go as hard as they did," he said, causing me to look at his ass like he was crazy.

"Bro, be honest with me. Did you fuck her?"

"Fuck who?" he asked.

"Stop playing fucking games. I'm talking about the bitch, Jasmine."

"Yeah, I fucked her, but that shit just happened. I had too much to drink, and I had no idea that I was going to end up at her place. By the time I realized that I had fucked up, it was too late."

"Damn! Are you still fucking with her, or was it just that night?" I asked, praying he wasn't still fucking with this girl.

"Well, I haven't fucked her again after that night, but I have been talking to her," he admitted.

"Is that who you're texting with right now?" I asked.

"Bro, I tried to leave her alone. I don't know what the fuck this girl did to my ass, but I can't seem to walk away."

"Well you're going to have to walk away because some bitch you just met isn't worth losing your wife and son," I pointed out, looking at his ass and shaking my head. "Man, don't tell me you let a bitch pussy whip your ass to the point to where you would risk what you have at home. Lah, if you fuck up again, you're going to lose her for good this time. I'm not trying to get all up in your business, but you and Chink fought too hard for this relationship for you to throw it away over some pussy. And yes, it's over some pussy because there's no way you got to know her ass in a matter of weeks."

"I hear you, bro, and trust, I have tried to walk away, but there's something about her that just keeps me wanting to know more about her."

"Ok bro, don't say that I didn't warn you because this shit is going to get ugly. This girl looks like trouble, and just by the stunt she pulled the other night, she wanted Chink to know, in her own way, that you two fucked already."

"Nah, she wouldn't do no shit like that. She knows that if Chink finds out it's a wrap, so she wouldn't risk it," he assured, sounding stupid and not like my brother at all.

I was ready to go because this was a waste of my time. I used to say all of the time that Lah would never settle down, and he proved me wrong and got married. I also used to say that he would never play the fool for any female, and he's about to prove me wrong again because this bitch is already playing with his fucking head, and she is going to cause him to lose everything. After I finished my first and last drink, I told him that I needed to go. I knew his ass wasn't going to go straight home, and I was just praying that Chink didn't call Polo because I really wanted no parts of this shit because it's just going to continue to cause problems in my relationship.

The last few weeks have been hell in my relationship due to Lah being a fuck up at home. Every night this week, Polo has been on the phone with Chink, either talking about what Lah was doing or what he wasn't doing, so I haven't been getting any love, and it was really starting to piss me off. His ass has even started to distance himself from me because he wasn't trying to hear my voice of reason. I don't know what this bitch's game was, but she was definitely playing a game with my brother, and his ass was too pussy whipped to see it.

Chapter Nine (Tasha)

"So you're hanging out with them again tonight?" Jasmine asked as she rolled her eyes.

"Yes, Jasmine. I told you that they invited me for a girl's night out."

"Well, why is it that every time they invite you out, they don't ask your best friend to hang out - for this girl's night or any of the others?" she asked.

"Jasmine, don't sit here and act as if you don't know why they didn't invite you. Did you forget what happened the first time you met them?"

"I'm just saying that if they don't like me enough to invite me to hang out with them, then you shouldn't hang out with them either. I'm your best friend, not them bitches," she exploded.

"Jasmine, what are we in high school now? We are all adults, and yes, you're my best friend, but that doesn't mean that I can't hang out with other females. Your ass is creeping with some new man, and you refuse to tell me who he is, but do you see me tripping?"

"That's different. I just met him, and all I'm doing is feeling him out right now. I don't even know if I will still be seeing him for much longer, but if I decide to, then you will be the first person I introduce him to," she said, trying to bullshit me.

"Look, I'm about to head out, so if it's not too late when I get home, I will give you a call." I was so ready for her to go.

"So you're kicking me out for your friends? It's fuck me, right?" she barked, copping an attitude.

"Jasmine, I told you that I was going out when you showed up unannounced, so why would you say that I'm kicking you out?"

"I never needed an invitation to come to my best friend's house before. Like you said, I didn't know that you had plans until I got here, so why don't you cancel and stay home so that we can watch movies and have a few drinks?" she asked.

"Jasmine, it's too late for me to cancel because I already said that I would go. I agreed to help drive, and they already booked the room, so I'm sorry. I can't cancel, but I promise we will do something next weekend, okay?"

"So this doesn't sound like a girl's night out. It sounds like you're going to be gone for the weekend."

"Yes, Jasmine, they invited me to go to Atlantic City for the weekend. Chink has been down, and Polo is taking her on a stress-free weekend away. She invited me, and I accepted. Can I go now?" I asked because she seemed to be stalling.

"Don't worry; I won't keep you from getting to your new friends any longer." She grabbed her bag and left without even saying goodbye or have a safe trip.

Jasmine was acting like a spoiled brat. I didn't know what the hell her problem was with Polo and Chink because neither one of them did anything to her. She was acting like she was all hurt by them not wanting to fuck with her, but she played herself by disrespecting Chink by dancing up on her man like that. Being she's my friend, I didn't put her on blast that night, but the next day I made it my business to tell her that she was wrong for doing that shit. I had to keep it real with her because if she could flirt with Chink's husband right in front of her, what do you think she would do with my husband, behind my back?

I saw that she was all up in Rellz's face that night too, and you better believe that I called her on that too. She had the nerve to say that she would never do any shit like that to me. I don't know how true it is, but trust, me telling her how I felt was her one and only warning. I love her to death, but there are a few things you don't fuck with when it comes to me - my children, my man, and any family that's bonded by blood. If she values our friendship, her ass better take heed to what I said to her.

I was driving my car to Chink's house and parking it in her garage because we all agreed on getting a rental for the drive to Atlantic City - something big enough for all of us. We would be picking up Polo once I got to Chink's house, and I invited my friend Kim, who lived in Jersey, so we would be picking her up on the way. Kim is a friend that I met at a book signing about two years ago in Newark. We had a lot in common, mainly books. We hit it off at the fair and have been friends ever since. We don't get to see each other a lot, so I couldn't wait until we picked her up because it's been about a month since the last time we met up in the city for dinner.

She and I will share one room, and Chink and Polo will share the other room. That worked out fine because we will have the chance to catch up on the latest books and talk about what's been going on in our worlds. I really needed this trip because, like I said earlier, I love Jasmine, but I needed a break away from her because, whenever she wasn't hanging out with her mystery man, her ass was popping up at my house without even calling first.

It took us about three hours to get to Atlantic City because of all the bathroom and food breaks. I think we still made good timing though, and Kim hit it off with Polo and Chink right away. That let me know that they were cool because Kim's ass always found something not to like about everybody. She keeps telling me that Jasmine means me no good, but I tried to tell her that Jasmine just has some issues so to know her is to love her, but she still isn't buying it. Once we checked in, we all agreed to shower, change, and meet up in the lobby in exactly one hour. I wanted to go and get my gamble on, but I knew that I wasn't down here to just gamble, so I had to keep an open mind that the others didn't just want to gamble. Shit, Rellz brought me to Atlantic City for a weekend last summer, and my ass has been hooked on gambling at the slot machines. Even though I didn't win, it was still fun, and my favorite slot machine was *Sex in the City*.

Kim and I were dressed and were now in the lobby waiting on Chink and Polo. We all decided that we were going to do some shopping, get something to eat, do some gambling, and then hit up a club for our first day here. We were staying at the Resorts, so we decided to just walk over to the Tanger Outlets. Now, how much shopping we were going to do, I didn't know, but I wasn't really up to carrying any bags. Our first stop was Nine West, and we were all up in there, getting our shoe shopping on. Chink had us cracking up, talking about how she wasn't paying those prices, and we needed to take her ass to Payless. I told her that Payless wasn't so damn cheap anymore, so she needed to just get some shoes, and get Payless out of her mind, because we weren't about to be shopping up in no damn Payless.

"Girl, you better get you a few of these shoes for our weekend because we will be hitting up at least three clubs on this visit," I said to her because she was still standing around like we were going to Payless.

"I'll tell you what. How about I pick one pair and rock them for the entire weekend?" she asked seriously, causing me to laugh at her ass.

"Okay, I guess that will work. Just as long as you don't take your ass over to no damn Payless," I laughed.

"Leave my sis alone, Tasha. This girl is just stuck in her ways, like she's not balling up in here," Polo explained.

"Yes, leave me alone. The less I spend in this damn store, the more I'll have to turn up in the casino," she said, laughing and causing us all to laugh.

We shopped for about another hour, making sure that we all had shoes and an outfit for the club tonight, before heading up the block to Ruby Tuesday to get something to eat. I wanted to hit up a few more stores but decided against it because I already had like four bags, and I refused to carry anymore. We ordered drinks and appetizers from the shareable menu. We got us some fire wings, fried mozzarella, spinach artichoke dip, and the thai phoon shrimp. It sounded like a lot, but shit, there were four of us, and my ass could eat.

"Jasmine was a little upset that she wasn't invited on this outing. She felt like if she wasn't invited, I should have declined," I said.

"Are you fucking serious? What would make her think that she would get an invite after the shit she pulled at your house?" Chink asked.

"Well, what in the hell happened at your house, and when, because you didn't tell me about it, Tasha?" Kim inquired.

"You know the get together that your ass failed to show up to," I reminded her.

"Girl, somebody better give me the tea. You know why my ass didn't show up. Stop playing, and spill it right now," she laughed.

"Jasmine was being very flirtatious with Chink's husband. She was dancing with her ass all up in his face. Chink and Polo were going to beat her ass, but I diffused the situation and got in Jasmine's ass later about it because you know I don't play that shit," I said.

"I have told you time and time again that her ass is not to be trusted, and you keep having her around Rellz's fine ass, being all fake and shit, calling him her brother. I don't like her, and I don't trust her ass," Kim announced.

"All I'm going to say to that is - if Jasmine has a death wish, that's on her. She was flirting with Rellz's ass too, but I didn't say anything to her until after the get together. She has been warned already, so if she decides to play with her life, that's on her," I said seriously.

"I'll drink to that because that's exactly how I feel about it. She has been warned," Chink agreed, and we all lifted our glasses.

After dinner, I was feeling a little toasty, but it wasn't going to stop me from shaking my ass, so while Chink and Polo went to the casino, I went to take a little nap. The club didn't start popping until like 1:00 am, so I'd be good to go by the time we left up out of this bitch. I didn't get to take my much-needed nap because Kim wanted to talk about Jasmine. She really wanted me to end my friendship with her because she said if she would disrespect Chink, right in her face, I didn't know what in the hell she would do behind my back. She also said that I needed to stop trusting her alone in my house with Rellz when I'm not home. I'm not going to lie, she had me thinking, but like I said, I had spoken my peace, and if Jasmine was a real friend, she would not cross that line. I called Rellz to check on him and the kids to make sure that he got them down okay before I hopped in the shower.

"Hey, babe. Did you get the kids down without any problems?" I asked when he picked up the phone.

"Tash, you know I'm a pro at this. Your man got this," he laughed.

"Yeah, okay. How long did it take you to get RJ down?" I laughed also because I knew that RJ gave his ass a hard time.

"Shit, I just got his ass down." We both laughed because RJ always gave his daddy a hard time when it was time to do anything with him.

"I'm about to head out to the club with the girls. I just wanted to call and check on you and the kids and to tell you that I love you."

"I love you too, Tash, and you better be good up in the club," he said.

"Always. I only have eyes for one man, and his name is Michael Ealy," I laughed.

"Don't get Michael Ealy fucked up," he said before ending the call.

We were all twisted leaving the club. I really had a good time. My ass danced all night, something that I hadn't done in a really long time. I'm glad that I decided not to listen to Jasmine and decided to hang out this weekend on this ladies getaway because it was definitely what I needed. Even Chink was stress-free and having a really good time. The best part about it was that we get to do it all over again tomorrow. We said our goodbyes, once we got off of the elevator, and entered our rooms that were located across from each other. I was too intoxicated to get into the shower out of fear that I would fall and hit my damn head. As soon as my head hit the pillow, I was out for the count.

Chapter Ten (Jasmine)

This is the third weekend that Tasha has left me hanging to hang out with her newfound friends, Chink and Polo. I'm really starting to think that she's trying to play me for these bitches that she's just met. When she left to go to Atlantic City with them, after I told her that I didn't think it was right of her to go if they couldn't invite me, I knew that the friendship wasn't going to be the same. Then she had the nerve to post pics on Facebook and Instagram of her fat friend, Kim, with the three of them, turning up. I'm can't lie; I was definitely starting to feel some type of way. So it was okay to invite Kim, but my ass wasn't invited? It's ok though; I've got something for all those bitches.

Chink's ass thought that she was pissing Lah off by going away for the weekend. NOT! His ass was at my house the entire weekend, chilling with me. At first I didn't think he was going to be able to pull it off because he was left with his son. What he did with his son, I didn't know, and I didn't care to ask because we spent the whole weekend fucking each other's brains out. He didn't even want to leave; I had to practically put his ass out. But since this bitch wants to try to take my friend from me, I'm going to show her how a real bitch plays at taking things.

"Hey, what are you doing?" I asked Lah when he picked up the phone.

"Chilling. What's up with you?" he responded.

"Nothing much. Just missing you and wishing you were here right now," I said.

"I'm missing you too, Ma. You saw that I wasn't trying to leave you the other day."

"So why don't you come by and chill? I promise to make it worth your while."

"And how do you plan on making it worth my while?" he asked, taking the bait.

"I can show you better than I can tell you, but keep in mind how this pussy felt the last time you were here. I promise you it's going to be ten times better this time around," I said, knowing that once he remembered how I had his ass feeling on his last visit, he wouldn't hesitate to get here.

"I'm on my way." He ended the call.

I knew it wouldn't take much convincing to get his ass to leave the house once I mentioned how good this pussy felt. I have pussy whipped many of men, but Lah was hooked after the first time we fucked. His stuck up ass wife must not be putting it on his ass the way she needed too. I really didn't want to invite him over with my daughter being home, but

I'm going to show that bitch of his that her nigga is mine now. Ariel usually sleeps through the night, but I couldn't say that she would tonight with the way my fuck sessions are set up, but I'm going to try my best not to wake her. If Ariel woke up, it would be a wrap because it's hard getting her down once she's up because she thinks it's playtime. I made sure that my bedroom was in tiptop order before I went to take a shower and get ready for Lah to come and give me what I yearn for just as much as he yearns for this pussy. I'm not going to front and say that I'm not feeling him because that would be far from the truth. I fell for his ass, just like he fell for me, but I'm not going to let him know how I feel about him because at the end of the day, he's still married. As pussy whipped as he is, it still doesn't mean that he would leave his wife for me because she does have the one thing that I don't, and that is his son.

Lah got to my house within an hour, and although I had sex on the brain, we did something that I never expected to do. We cuddled up in bed, and I laid in his arms as we watched movies and just kicked it. I'm not going to lie; it felt hella good. We talked about everything. He told me that he and Chink had a son named LJ, and he said that they had a rough year before they were married. He didn't really go into details, and I was happy about that because I didn't tell him about my ex and why I didn't have a boyfriend because, although he opened up a little to me, I just wasn't ready to let him know that the man that I loved was in love with another man, who happened to be my best friend. Shit, niggas freak out about that homo bullshit, so I wasn't ready for him to run away right now because of my past.

We kicked it for hours with him telling me that he had to go like every thirty minutes, but we continued to watch movies until we both dozed off. The vibrating of his phone woke me up, but he didn't budge. I looked at the clock, and it was four in the morning, so I knew that it was no one but his wife calling him. I ignored the vibrating phone and refused to wake him up as I laid my head back on my pillow and pushed my ass into his groin, falling back to sleep with a smile on my face.

"Jasmine. Jasmine, get up," I heard Lah say as he shook me lightly.

"Hey, I'm up. What happened?" I asked, trying to adjust my eyes to the sunlight that was coming in from the window.

"I overslept. It's seven in the morning, and I have to get home to shower and get ready for work. My wife is going to have a fit. I promised not to stay out all night again," he said, causing me to smile on the inside because, even though I didn't get any dick, my mission was accomplished.

"I'm sorry. I fell asleep too."

"It's okay. It's not your fault. I should have set my alarm," he said, kissing me on my lips.

I walked him downstairs so that I could lock the door. I gave him another kiss before letting him leave and told him to make sure that he called me on his lunch break later on. After my door was locked, I went back upstairs to get another hour of sleep before Ariel decided to get up.

Chapter Eleven (Chink)

I sat up all night waiting for Lah to bring his ass home. He told me that he was stepping out to go to the store and that he would be right back. His ass has been gone all night; I called him and even texted him, and he still refused to answer. He promised that he wouldn't do this stupid shit anymore, and I was just about tired of him. There's no way that he can tell me that he isn't fucking around on me because all the signs point to another woman. I knew that he would be bringing his ass home soon because he had to be to work at 9:00 a.m., which meant that he's going to come in with some lame excuse and say that he can't talk because he has to go to work. His ass didn't have to worry about coming up with an excuse because I wasn't going to ask him not one fucking question about where the fuck he was. I made sure to have LJ in the bed with me, and my bedroom door locked, so whatever the fuck he was wearing, he would have to wear that shit to work because I would not be opening my door for his ass.

When he didn't bring his ass home, I already knew that I wasn't going to work, and LJ wasn't going to school. I was in a fucked up mood, and I wasn't going to be entertaining anyone today. I called Polo last night and even had her have Liem call him because, at first, I was worried that something happened to him because he said that he was going to the store, and being the store was only about twenty minutes away, I just knew something happened to his ass. So when he didn't answer for Liem, I just chalked that shit up as he was playing me again and was laid up with some bitch.

It was now going on 9:30, and he still had yet to show. I picked up the phone and called Liem to ask him if Lah was at work, and when he said that he was, I was floored. I didn't even respond as the tears fell, and I ended the call. I just didn't understand what was happening to us or what had happened to the man that I fell in love with. We were doing just fine up until the night he went to Rellz's club. My gut was telling me that the other woman was Tasha's friend, Jasmine, but I didn't have any proof. I have never been one to snoop before, but it was time to do some investigating because I'd be damned if I let that bitch, or any bitch, come and fuck up what we had.

I went into the bathroom to wash my face and brush my teeth so that I could fix LJ some breakfast. After I put the sausages on, I grabbed my phone to call him, just to see if he would pick up the phone, and he sent me to voicemail. I could have called him at work, but I refused to go to that extreme because, with the way that I was feeling, he would have lost his job today. Once LJ was fed, I told him to go into his room and play because I needed to be alone to think without him asking me question after question.

I had been moping around the house all day, trying to figure out what I was going to say to Lah when he finally walked through the door. I prepared myself for the lie that I knew he was going to come up with because, whatever he told me, I was going to have to play along and make him think that shit was good because I had something for his ass. If he wanted to start treating me like he was fucking with a stupid bitch, I was going to start acting like one until I caught his ass, and trust, when I do, his ass better hope like hell I don't send him to his fucking grave. I called Polo up to let her know not to even question Liem about whether or not Lah told him about his whereabouts because it wasn't necessary. Once I let her in on what I had planned, she was game.

"Babe, before you go off on me, just let me explain what happened," Lah said once he got home from work.

"I'm listening." I prepared myself for the bullshit and prayed that I would be able to hold my tongue.

"When I left to go to the store yesterday, Rellz called me to let me know that his pops was having some problems with some dude, and he needed him. So, he asked me if I could meet him, and being I was already in the streets, I headed to

72

his pop's house. Long story short, the shit got out of hand with dude, and his pops put hands on him. In turn, the dude's wife called the cops, and they arrested his pops, so I was up at the jail with him all night. His pops was released at like eight this morning, so instead of coming home, I went straight to work from there," he explained with a straight fucking face.

I counted backwards from ten because I really wanted to go in on his ass, but I knew I needed to keep my cool. Men just didn't know how to lie. First off, his dumb ass knows that I'm friends with Rellz's wife, so a phone call to her would have blown up his spot because, had he wanted to cover his ass, he would have ran his story by Rellz. When I spoke to Tasha last night, Rellz was home so for him to start lying, and doing it recklessly, tells me that he's creeping.

"Lah, we had this conversation before, and you promised. I know that shit happens, so all I ask is for a phone call, letting me know something. When you don't answer my calls or texts, I worry, and it's not a good feeling not knowing if your husband is laid up somewhere hurt," I said, pissed off on the inside.

"Babe, there was just so much going on that it slipped my mind to even give you a call, and I do apologize."

"I guess it's cool. I'm just glad that you're okay," I said.

"Thanks, babe. I'm going to go up and say what's up to LJ before taking a shower."

"Okay, I will be in the kitchen starting dinner," I replied.

Once in the kitchen, the tears fell. I just couldn't believe that he looked me in my face and lied. The fact that he changed overnight hurts me so bad. I mean we weren't perfect, but we were better than this shit right here. I knew that I was losing him slowly because he never disrespected me the way he's disrespecting me now. I even saw that he had started to become distant from LJ, and that had never happened before. When he was at home, and not at work, it was always about LJ, whether they were in the backyard, shooting hoops, or sitting and watching a kid flick, he did it. Now all LJ's gets is a simple, "What's up, little man?" and that's it. He doesn't even spend time with me like he used to because all I ever see him do is stay up on his damn phone, and when I asked him about it, he tells me that he's playing Criminal Case. I wiped at my tears and decided to just get dinner cooked and over with because it really was no sense in crying when his ass didn't seem to care if I was alright anymore.

~

I'd just left the shop and was on my way to meet up with Tasha because I needed to talk to her about what I've been feeling lately. Polo wasn't able to go with me because she had to work the overnight shift tonight. When I got to the mall, Tasha was sitting outside of Haagen-Dazs like she said she would be.

"Hey, girl. Thanks for meeting up with me on a weeknight." I greeted her with a hug.

"No problem; anytime, girl. So, what's up?" she asked me.

"I wouldn't have called, but I can't continue to hold this in," I said, taking a seat.

"It's okay. Just talk to me, Chink."

"I think that your friend, Jasmine, is sleeping with my husband," I blurted out.

"Are you serious? What makes you think that she's sleeping with him?" she asked.

"Well, just like any other relationship, mine wasn't perfect, but Lah has never stayed out all night or looked me in my face and lied to me until he went to your husband's club and met her ass. I may be wrong, but my gut is telling me that she's the woman that has my husband acting brand new," I explained.

"All I know is that she has been seeing some mystery man, and when I ask her about it, she tells me that she's not ready to share until she knows where the relationship is going." Tasha paused like she was thinking about something.

"Do you think that her mystery man is Lah? I know that's your best friend, but if she's messing with my husband, I'm going to body that bitch."

"I'm hoping that's not the case because that would be fucked up on so many levels. Not only because he's married, but also because she knows that I don't get down like that and wouldn't continue being someone's friend if that person slept with a married man. I know that some females wouldn't agree with breaking off a friendship for that reason, because it's not their husband or boyfriend, but I look at it like this, if she would fuck with your husband, she would fuck with mine," she said, getting pissed.

"And that's exactly how I feel about the situation."

"So, what's the plan?" she asked.

"I was thinking about maybe following his ass when he left the house, but I know that my ass would get caught before he made it to his destination. So, the only logical thing to do is hire someone to do it for me."

"Yeah, that sounds like a plan, but don't hire an amateur. Get one of those private investigators to do the shit. At least you know the shit will be done right," she suggested.

"Well, I'm going to call a few places tomorrow to see if I can get someone to take the job because if he is, in fact, cheating, I need to know who the bitch is and handle it accordingly before she ruins my marriage." Looking at Tasha, I continued. "So, I'm going to call you if I get someone to do it, and all I ask is that you don't mention this to Jasmine because if you do, and she is the person he's cheating with, both of them are going to fall back."

"You don't have to worry about me saying anything to anyone. Just like you, I want to know if she's capable of doing something like this, so I promise she will not get a heads up from me."

"Thank you. The only other person that will know will be Polo, and that's it. So, I'm going to go and get out of here. Thanks again for coming to meet me," I said, standing up and giving her a hug.

"No problem. I just hope that my friend, or anyone for that matter, isn't cheating with your husband." She hugged me back before leaving.

When I got home, Lah was sitting on the sofa. I walked over and greeted him with a kiss. His facial expression told me that he was upset that I got home late, but for the life of me, I didn't understand why because this wasn't my first time getting home late. He knew that sometimes the last client goes past the time that I leave to come home.

"I didn't know that you were going to be coming home late tonight," he stated.

"Well, you know I never plan on coming home late, but my last client's hair took longer than I expected. I knew that me being late wouldn't be a problem because you were picking LJ up today," I said.

"And you couldn't call?" he asked.

"No, I didn't call because I didn't feel the need to call. If I wasn't home yet, you already knew that I was still at the shop, working," I said, trying my best not to get pissed off.

"If you didn't call and tell me that you were at the shop and that you were going to be late, how was I supposed to know where you were?"

I looked at him like, 'Are you fucking serious?' Was his ass really questioning my whereabouts? Have I ever given him a reason to question anything that I've told him? Hell no, and I didn't appreciate how he was coming at me because, whether he wanted to admit it or not, he knows that my ass isn't creeping on him. So he had to just be fucking with me because he was in a fucked up mood and taking it out on me.

"Well, I was at the shop, and I didn't have time to stop what I was doing to call you because I was trying to finish my client's hair and get home." I spoke a little louder than I intended to.

"Yeah, okay, if you say so. You want me to call you every second of the fucking day when I'm out, but you don't do that shit in return, so how do I know that you are where the fuck you say you are?" he barked.

"Are we really about to do this right now, Lah?"

"Do what right now? Aren't you the one always bitching with a nigga when he doesn't call, but it's okay for your ass to be late and not call? I just want to make sure that we're on the same page because, if you're going to get at me about not calling, I just want you to remember that you do the same shit, so don't sweat me when I do it."

"You're right, Lah. I should have called to let you know that I was running late. I apologize," I said, rolling my eyes and walking into the kitchen.

His little fucking girlfriend must have pissed him off, and now, he's taking that shit out on me, but it's okay. I made dinner and left him to fix himself and LJ a plate because I needed a hot shower ASAP.

"So you're not going to sit down and have dinner with me and your son?" he asked.

"I want to get out of these clothes and take a shower. I'll eat later," I answered.

"You sure you were at work and not with some nigga? You never wanted to take a shower before sitting down and having dinner with us," he accused.

"Lah, you know, just like I know, that I wasn't with no fucking nigga because that's not what I do. If I didn't want to be with you, I wouldn't be with you," I said.

"Yeah, okay. Let me find out otherwise, and it's going to be a problem," he said.

I'm getting so tired of him threatening me about what he's going to do if he finds out that I'm messing with another man. His ass better be worried about what I'm going to do if I find out that he's messing with that bitch, Jasmine, or any other bitch for that matter. I just ignored his ass and went to take a shower. The shower could have waited, but I didn't want to sit down and have dinner with his ass. Before getting in the shower, I had to call Polo to let her know how this nigga just came at me.

"Hey, girl. What's up?" she said, answering the call.

"Your fucking brother has been getting on my nerves, since I walked in this fucking door, because I was late."

"He's not my brother anymore until he get his shit together, and he has a lot of fucking nerve. Tell his ass that at least you brought your ass home," she said.

"My point exactly, and he went off when I said that I wasn't ready to eat and just wanted to take a shower."

"You know when a nigga starts cheating, he automatically starts to accuse his girlfriend or his wife, just based on his guilty ass. Tell Lah to kick fucking rocks."

"I'm not paying his ass no fucking mind, but girl, let me go and get in this shower. I just needed to vent because this nigga is really taking me through it."

"Don't sweat anything his ass is saying right now because like I said, that's how a guilty nigga acts. We both know that you're not fucking with anybody else, so don't let him get to you. Go and take your shower, and call me if you need to vent again."

"Thanks, sis."

"No problem. That's what I'm here for," she said, ending the call.

Chapter Twelve (Polo)

Today has been a trying day because Paris has been crying all day long, and I was just about ready to pull my hair out. Liem was at work, so I tried to chalk it up to her just having a cranky morning, but by noon, she was still in distress, so I called a cab and took her to the emergency room. I tried to get an emergency appointment with her doctor but was unable to because her ass wasn't in today. I really hated that I had to come to this hospital. My crying baby and I had been here for an hour, and she had only been in triage. I called Liem to let him know that he was going to have to come and pick me and Paris up from the hospital when he got off work because I was positive that we would still be here. By the time we were called to the back, I was pissed the hell off and even more pissed that my baby had an ear infection. They gave her a dose of antibiotics and some pain medication in the hospital, and they gave me a prescription to fill after I left the hospital.

My baby was now sleeping peacefully in my arms as we waited for Liem to come and pick us up. I was hoping like hell that he would hurry up because there was this little boy who just kept running and screaming, making so much noise like he wasn't in a hospital waiting area; his ass must have thought that he was at the park. I was praying that his little ass didn't wake Paris up because I was trying to keep her asleep at least until we made it back home. Paris being sick this morning had me doing a lot of thinking today about what I wanted and needed to do for the wellbeing of my child.

No, this little fucking boy didn't just throw his fucking toy, almost hitting my fucking daughter. I waited a few minutes to see if his mother was going to intervene because everyone in the waiting area saw that this toy almost hit my baby.

"Excuse me. Can you please get your son?" I asked his mother or whoever the fuck she was.

The bitch had the nerve to look in front of her, look to the side of her, and finally behind her before responding. This bitch here wanted to try me; I could feel it.

"Are you talking to me?" she asked, rolling her eyes.

"If this is your son, then yes, I'm talking to you. He almost hit my daughter with his toy." I was trying to keep calm because her whole stance was pissing me off.

"Jaden, get your ass over here before I have to fuck somebody up in this fucking hospital," she yelled out instead of apologizing and making her bad ass son sit down.

"Look, all of that wasn't even necessary. All you had to do was get your son. This isn't a fucking playground; it's the fucking hospital with sick fucking kids who don't need to be ducking and dodging toys that your son is throwing all over the place," I said, a little too loud, waking up my fucking baby.

I swear; I wish that I hadn't come to the fucking city hospital. This fucking hospital was a joke, right along with the fucking security. He saw this bad ass motherfucking kid running around like he was in the park and annoying everyone, and he didn't say shit. I know one thing; if that bitch said one more fucking word, I was going to sit Paris on the fucking chair and kick her ass.

Liem walked through the door just in time because I was ready to snatch those nappy ass-fucking braids out of her head. She must have felt some kind of way when she saw that Liem was with me because she whispered to her friend, "Look at this sell-out nigga," but I heard her. I wanted so bad to run up on that bitch, but I just couldn't do it with my daughter present. It was bad enough that she heard me cursing - something I tried hard not to do in front of her. They pick up on stuff at such an early age, and I didn't want my baby's first words being one of my bad words.

"Punk ass bitch," I said once Liem and Paris were out of earshot.

All she saw was a white girl, so she thought I was going to back down. NOT! I stayed in the door of the hospital for a few minutes, just to see if she was going to continue to pop off, but she tended to her son - something her ass should have done from the beginning because, had that toy hit my baby, I was going to jail. Liem drove to the pharmacy to get Paris' prescription filled, while I stayed in the car with her. She was back to sleeping peacefully, so I didn't want to take her out of her seat to go inside. It was so hard trying to get her to sleep today, and now I felt kind of bad that I complained about her crying now that I knew that she was crying because she wasn't feeling well. When she wakes up, I'm going to make sure to give her a million and one kisses all over her little chubby face. Once at home, I woke her up to give her a bath to wash that dirty hospital experience off of her. She didn't want her bottle, so I just gave her the next dose of the antibiotic and a little Motrin and put her back to sleep.

I went to join Liem in the living room. I needed to make this conversation quick because he was watching Bones, and I hated this show with a passion. Liem always tells me that he didn't understand how I couldn't watch Bones but could sit and watch Grey's Anatomy and not flinch once at the scenes. Watching Grey's Anatomy didn't bother me the way Bones did; why I didn't know, but then again maybe it had something to do with me not wanting to take my eyes off of the show because of Derek Shepherd's fine ass.

"Hey, babe. I need to run something by you real quick. Real quick," I repeated, looking at the screen with disgust at the scene that was now showing.

"What's up?" he said, laughing.

"I've been thinking about something today that I really want you to take into consideration."

"I'm listening," he said.

"I was thinking about quitting my job and being a stay at home mom until Paris reaches school age because today was kind of a wake-up call that I need to be home with my baby. Had I not been home today, that would have been the babysitter caring for her while she was sick when it should have been me. I also want to finally take the lessons to get my driver's license because I'm tired of waiting on you to always have to take me somewhere or pick me up. Oh, and when I get my license, you have to buy me a car," I added.

"Polo, before we even had Paris I told you that you didn't have to go to work because I just wanted you to concentrate on school. And how many times did I tell you to let me teach you to drive and you backed out? If you're serious about learning, I'm your guy, and I would love for you to be home with Paris. You know I wasn't really feeling the whole family daycare thing to begin with," he said.

"So what kind of car are you going to buy me?" I asked, laughing.

"Let's work on getting you these lessons and you passing the road test before you start worrying about what kind of car you're going to get," he laughed.

"I'm going upstairs to call my manager on his emergency line and let him know that I will not be returning. This is considered an emergency, isn't it?" I laughed, happy that I wouldn't be returning.

Chapter Thirteen (Chink)

I sat staring at the envelope that I picked up from the private investigator earlier, and my nerves were all over the place. He told me that his clients usually sit with him and go over the contents of his findings, but I told him that it wasn't necessary because I didn't want to be all up in my feelings in his office. I was waiting on Tasha and Polo to get to my house before opening the envelope because I didn't want to be alone. Also, I needed someone to keep my ass out of jail if something was in this envelope that proved that his ass was, in fact, cheating.

The investigator did tell me that there were findings, but I was praying that he was just talking to a chick or some shit like that because I could deal with that. I didn't even get to go out and celebrate last week with Polo and Liem on her passing her road test because my nerves have been all over the place. I just knew that I wouldn't have been able to concentrate on having a good time, so I told her that I would make it up to her, and she said that she understood.

Tasha and Polo finally got to my house, and I was ready to get this shit over with because the not knowing was killing me. Lah wasn't home; he said that he was going to hang out after work with a couple of dudes from his job. I didn't even put up a fuss about it because him not being home worked for me. We all sat, staring at the envelope, like it was going to open itself. I picked up the envelope, and my hand started to shake; I was so nervous. I needed to calm myself down, put my big girl panties on, and open the damn envelope.

I opened the envelope and dumped out everything that was inside onto the table. I was floored as I saw picture after picture of Lah entering Jasmine's house. A couple of other pictures showed him and Jasmine leaning against his car, with her standing in between his leg, kissing. I felt sick as I continued to look at the rest of the pictures, showing all types of public affection, like he didn't have a fucking wife at home. I continued to look at the pictures, and I had to be honest; I was hurt and embarrassed. I wanted to cry so badly, but I fought hard to keep my tears at bay because I didn't want them to know how much the shit hurt me.

"Damn, why Lah? I knew he was fucking up lately, but I honestly didn't think that he was fucking around with this bitch." Polo said, pissed off.

"I'm going to fucking kill this motherfucker in his sleep. After all that I do, and have done, for his ass, he's going to disrespect me and cheat on me with this bitch after he told me that he wasn't. He looked me right in my fucking face and lied to me," I yelled, not caring if I woke LJ up because that's how pissed off I was, and before I knew it, the tears came.

"Listen, Chink. Let me just say that I know that you haven't known me long, but I'm going to speak from experience. I used to be the type of bitch that shot first and asked questions later, but since I had my daughter, I try my best to let logic play a part in most of my decisions. Jasmine is my best friend, so I know the best way to get back at her. Trust me when I tell you that all you have to do is have Lah break it off with her in front of you. I know it sounds high school, but trust me; it will hurt her more than you beating her ass. And once I cut her ass off, that's going to take her over the top, and that's all the payback you need. Now, how you choose to deal with Lah, that's on you because I couldn't begin to give advice on how to handle your husband because, at the end of the day, you have to live with your decision," Tasha said.

I sat quietly for a few seconds, considering what she was saying. It made some sense, and it would definitely keep me out of jail, but I'm not going to lie; I felt a whole lot better when I thought about just getting a gun and shooting Lah and that bitch, Jasmine, right between the fucking eyes. But when reality set in, I had to think about what would happen to LJ if I killed his father because not only would he not have his father, he wouldn't have his mother because I would be sitting in a jail cell. I needed to really take some time and think about what I wanted to do; I had to decide if I was going to really consider staying with his lying, cheating ass.

Once Polo and Tasha left, I took the envelope upstairs and hid it under the mattress on my side of the bed until I was ready to show him. I wanted to give him the benefit of the doubt and see if he was going to continue to look me in my face and lie. His ass didn't stay out all night, but he did get home after midnight. I know that he was shocked to see me up and reading on my Kindle. He said that he was going to take a shower, and I didn't say anything; I just kept my eyes on the Kindle, ignoring his ass. He knew that I was upset, but he probably thought that I was upset about him coming home late. He walked out of the bathroom, and I almost forgot that he was a lying, cheating dog as I looked at how good he looked wrapped only in a towel. I diverted my stare because I had to stay focused and get through this conversation without ending up on all fours with him fucking the shit out of me.

"What are you still doing up, babe?" he asked me.

"I was waiting on you to get home because I need to talk to you," I said with my lip trembling.

"What's wrong, babe? Talk to me." Lah had a worried look on his face.

"I need to ask you something, and I need you to tell me the truth," I said, sitting up in bed and putting my Kindle down.

"What is it?" he asked, stuttering a little.

"I know I asked you this already, but I'm going to ask you again. Are you sleeping with that girl, Jasmine?" I asked, holding my breath and hoping that he told me the truth.

He sat up in the bed and put his head in his hands, and although I already knew the truth, it didn't stop me from wanting to bash his fucking head in as his body language answered my question. I wasn't letting his ass off the hook; he needed to look me in my face and verbally answer the question.

"Chink, I'm sorry," he said.

"Lah, I need you to look me in my face and tell me what the fuck you're sorry for." My tears began to fall as he lifted his head out of his hands.

"Chink, I'm sorry. It just happened one time - the night that I didn't come home from the club," he said, continuing to lie.

I didn't even have the energy to sit and argue with him or go back and forth about how many times he fucked the bitch because I just felt myself getting angry. Instead of verbally telling him that he was a fucking liar, I just got up off the bed, put my hand under the side that I was sitting on, pulled out the envelope, and handed it to him. I watched as he looked at me with questioning eyes before opening the envelope. When he pulled the first picture out, his ass had that I fucked up look on his face.

"Why, Lah? So this is how you're doing it now, cheating with a random bitch that you met in a club?" I asked him.

"Listen, Chink. I had too much to drink that night. I wasn't thinking straight."

"So what's your excuse for all the other times you fucked that bitch? The part that's really fucking with me is that you looked me right in my fucking face and lied. You were all up in my ear about what you would do to me and the next nigga if you found out that I was cheating when you're the one out here getting your fucking dick wet. So what the fuck should I do to you and that bitch?" His nonchalant attitude was pissing me off; he was acting like getting drunk and fucking someone else was okay.

"Chink, I said I'm sorry. I promise you that she means nothing to me. I love you, and I fucked up. Again, I'm sorry," he said.

"Really that bitch didn't mean anything to you? I can't tell because, if that bitch meant nothing to you, you wouldn't be all up in those pictures, showing public affection like she was your wife. If she meant nothing to you then you would have been just fucking that bitch and bringing your ass home. But that wasn't the case. You were fucking her and staying at her house like that's where the fuck you laid your head every night."

"Chink, I know I fucked up. Just tell me what I need to do to fix this. I swear on my mom's grave that it will never happen again. Please believe me," he begged. He was trying to pull me in his arms, and I snatched away from his ass.

"No, since you were treating me, your fucking wife, like the fucking side chick and that hoe bitch like your wife, go take your cheating ass to her fucking house. I'm good over here, nigga," I yelled as I tried to calm myself down because the more hyped I got, the more the devil was telling me to cut his ass.

"I wasn't treating her like my fucking wife. You're my wife, and I love you. That bitch doesn't hold a candle to you. Like I said, I fucked up, thinking with the wrong head."

"I can't tell because you were lying to me practically every fucking day to go lay with her ass, and trust that I don't need you to tell me that she doesn't hold a candle to my ass because I already know that shit. The only motherfucker that acts like he doesn't know is your punk ass because you're the one that put that basic bitch on a pedestal when you have all of this at home. I'm sure the next man will appreciate me and know my worth."

"Chink, don't get fucked up. Now I said that I was fucking sorry, so don't be throwing the next nigga up in my face," he said, trying to cop an attitude.

"Nigga, are you fucking serious right now? You just got caught with your motherfucking pants down, and you're telling me that I can't talk about the next nigga. Fuck you. Maybe I can go sit on Rellz's fucking lap and see how the fuck you feel then," I said, and before I knew it, he had slapped the shit out of me.

"Oh shit. I'm sorry, babe. I didn't mean to hit you. That shit just caught me off guard," he said, attempting to rub my face.

"So that's how you're doing it now, Lah? Putting your fucking hands on me. I know you don't have a fucking death wish, so I advise you to keep your fucking hands to yourself. If you ever put your fucking hands on me again, I will kill you in your fucking sleep," I hissed, meaning every word.

"Babe, I would never hit you; that shit you said just caught me off guard. I'm sorry," he said, putting his head back into his hands.

I wanted him to hold me because it hurt so badly, and at the end of the day, I still loved my husband, and I knew in my heart that I wasn't leaving him. I also knew that he didn't mean to hit me because he wasn't that type of man. He fucked up, had a weak moment, and lost his fucking mind in the process, but like I said before, I loved him and I refused to leave him so that she could have him. I'm going to take Tasha's advice and have his ass tell Jasmine that he needed to talk to her, and when they meet up, my ass will be right there so he can tell that bitch to kick fucking rocks. I'm not going to put my hands on the bitch as long as she understood that whatever they had was over.

"Lah, if you want a second chance at this marriage, you need to let that bitch know that it's over," I stated.

"I do want another chance at our marriage. I love you, and I made the biggest mistake of my life. I'm going to make it up to you; I promise."

"Show me how sorry you are by calling that bitch and letting her know that you need to meet with her. When you go to meet her, I will be right there with you so that we can tell her in her face together as husband and wife. Make sure that you tell her to meet you somewhere other than her house," I said.

I watched as he picked up his phone and called her and told her exactly what I told him to tell her, minus the part about me being there. My heart was heavy, and I swear that I tried hard not to cry because I have been told by Polo plenty of times that I needed to man up and stop crying all of the time, but if anybody has ever been hurt by a cheating partner, you know how much this shit hurts. I was always sensitive to a lot of things growing up, and now that I'm grown, that fact still remains about me.

"After we meet with this bitch, make sure you change your phone number, too," I demanded.

"I will, babe, and thanks for giving me another chance to make this right," he replied.

I know some of you think that I let him off too easily, but at the end of the day, he's my husband, and I believe that he deserves a second chance to make things right. Shit, we all have weak moments, and had I not befriended Tasha, I might have fucked her husband too, so shit does happen because temptation is a motherfucker. I told him that he was still in the doghouse, so he had to sleep on the couch until I felt comfortable with him sleeping in my bed again. He wasn't too happy, but he took his ass downstairs, and when he was gone, I cried myself to sleep.

When I woke up, I watched as Lah got ready for work. He told me that Jasmine called him and told him that she wasn't able to meet him at the place they agreed on, so he had to meet her at her house. I told him that when he got off of work we would meet at home and then drive over to her house together. I didn't want to go to her house, but it is what it is. I will just have to have Polo get LJ for me today. I couldn't even concentrate at work today because my mind was on how this meeting was going to play out and how she was going to feel when she saw me at the door with Lah. I let Tasha know that we were meeting at Jasmine's house tonight, and she told me that she was going to let Jasmine know that she could no longer fuck with her. I appreciated her for not wanting to fuck with Jasmine anymore, but I had to say that if it had been Polo, who messed with a married man, I don't think it would have been that easy for me to cut her off.

When Lah pulled up to Jasmine's house, I was nervous, not because I was scared, but I was worried that I would jump on the bitch. I stood behind him as he rang the doorbell. When she opened up the door, she went to hug him, but he kind of pushed her back. When I walked in behind him, the look on her face was priceless.

"What's going on?" she asked.

"Yo, Jas, I just asked you to meet with me so that I could tell you to your face that this shit is over. My wife knows everything, and she's here so that you know this shit is for real," he stated.

"So all the talk about being with me was bullshit?" she asked.

"I'm married, so all that talk about being with you was just that – talk," he answered.

"Are you serious?" she asked, looking like she was about to cry.

"Yes, I'm serious, so I'm going to need you to lose my number and not try to contact me. I'm sorry if it sounds harsh, but I love my wife and my son. I know that I fucked up, but I'm going to make this shit right."

"So you're just like all the other men, right? Feeding me bullshit, just to get what you want. I opened up to you, something I haven't done with anyone in a long time. I fell in love with you, and I thought you were falling in love with me too," she cried.

"Shorty, I'm sorry if I misled you. Yes, I cheated on my wife, but I will never love another woman. It was just sex for me."

"So it was just sex? No need to lie because your wife is standing here. You know, just like I know, that you were falling for me just like I fell for you. Keep it real. If it was just sex for you, we wouldn't have been laying up all those nights, watching movies and just hanging out. Most nights we didn't even have sex, so stop fronting," she said, causing me to feel some kind of way.

I knew there was some truth to what she was saying. His ass was feeling her because, if he wasn't, he would have been bringing his ass home after hitting, but no, he was playing fucking house with this bitch. I understood where she was coming from and how she felt that he played her, but all of that didn't matter right now because he said that he's done so them going back and forth about it wasn't going to change the fact that he's leaving with me and leaving her ass alone.

"Look, Jasmine, it really doesn't matter what he felt for you because the shit is over. He just told you that he loves his wife and his son, so I'm going to need you to respect that and not contact my husband any further," I said, wrapping this shit up.

"This has nothing to do with you. I wasn't fucking you; I was fucking Lah," she said.

"It has everything to do with me. This is my husband, and when you decided to deal with a married man, you involved me, so I'm telling you to stay the fuck away from my husband."

"Lah, look me in my face and tell me that it's over. Tell me that you felt nothing for me, and I will respect your wishes." She grabbed Lah's face, basically ignoring what I had just said.

Lah grabbed both of her hands and looked her in her face. He told her that it was over and that he never loved her because he loved me. He told her that he apologized if he made her feel as if they were going to be together because that was never his intention. I could tell that he was hurt that he had to do this to her in front of me because I'm no fool; he was feeling her, just not enough to lose me. I grabbed at his arm, letting him know that it was time to go because seeing him looking as if he was hurt, kind of hurt me. She was screaming and asking him to please not do this to her. She got down on her knees, crying out to him. I felt bad for her as we walked out of the door, but these females need to stop messing with married men, thinking that they're going to leave their wives for them. Even though he said what he had to say to her, I felt it in my gut that she wasn't going to just walk away.

Chapter Fourteen (Tasha)

I really hate what I'm about to do, but it has to be done. I'm also kind of upset with myself because I have always listened to my gut feeling. It was screaming, telling me that something wasn't right about Jasmine; I should have trusted my feelings and kept it pushing because I wouldn't be in this situation right now. I can't stand a disloyal bitch, and it was time for me to clean house. Only loyal bitches can be around me and be called my friend. I pulled up to the mall because that's where I was meeting her at since she was no longer invited to my house. I sat down outside of the food court, waiting for her to arrive.

While I waited, I called to see how Chink was doing. She had told me before that she hadn't allowed Lah out of the doghouse just yet, but he had been bringing his ass home. My call went to voicemail, but it was okay because I saw Jasmine approaching me. I got up so that we could go into the food court and grab a seat to get this shit over with.

"Hey, Diva. What's up?" she asked, like she didn't fucking know that Chink told me what the fuck was up.

"Well, you know that Chink told me that you were sleeping with Lah. You already know where I stand with females that I can't trust," I started.

"Tasha, what does me fucking Lah have to do with you? I just don't understand how you've just met this fucking girl, and you're riding with the bitch. I have been your girl way before Chink was in the picture," she said.

"I may have just met her, but my morals haven't changed. I don't fuck with females that I can't trust. When I asked you if you were messing with Lah, you looked me dead in my face and told me that you weren't. I can't stand a liar, and I most definitely can't stand a female that sleeps with men that belong to someone else. So with that being said, we can no longer be friends because who's to say that you won't be pushing up on my husband next," I said, deciding not to sugarcoat the shit.

"Tasha, are you fucking serious right now? So you're going to end our friendship because of who I'm fucking. You're sitting here talking about loyalty, but where is your loyalty to me? You don't even know that bitch, and let's not get shit twisted like you've never slept with another man before behind your husband's back."

"I don't have to know her. To be honest, it could have been a stranger in the street. The point that I'm trying to make to you is that I don't rock with shady ass females. So, if that stranger that I never met was married, and you were fucking with her husband on the low, I would feel the same way. I'm a firm believer of if you did it to that person, you will do the same shit to me because what will make me off limit? And as far as me sleeping with another man behind my husband's back, that doesn't have anything to do with me sleeping with someone's husband," I said, getting pissed off that she brought that shit up.

"Well, Tasha, if that's the way you feel, then it's whatever. I'm not about to sit here and beg you to be my fucking friend because you're not a real friend any fucking way. You're a fucking hypocrite. If you're so fucking hell bent on loyalty, why the fuck is Rellz still sleeping in your fucking bed?" the bitch had the nerve to say.

"Jasmine, I'm not about to go there with you because you can sit here and throw stones all fucking day if you'd like, but the fact still remains that we are no longer friends. So I advise you to leave before I forget that we are in a public place, and let it do what it do."

"Whatever, bitch. You don't fucking scare me. I've got something for all of you motherfuckers. Just watch and see," she said, getting up from the table.

I don't take too lightly to threats, but I let the bitch have that because she was upset. If she had said something like it had nothing to do with him being married, just maybe I would have considered still being her friend. Sometimes you can't help who you fall for, but the bitch wasn't remorseful, so this was definitely something that she would do again, and I just couldn't risk having her around my husband anymore. I know that some would say that I wasn't a real friend because a real friend wouldn't have just cut off someone that they were rocking with for over two years, but I'm a different bitch, cut from a different cloth.

I didn't even get in the door good before my phone started ringing. It was Kim calling. Her ass timed me good. I told her that I was going to call her because it was only going to take me about an hour. She could have waited for me to call her ass.

"Damn, were you sitting by the clock?" I asked her, laughing.

"Nah, I was actually watching the time on the cable box. Now tell me what you said to that bitch," she laughed.

"You really hate her that much that you get off on me losing a friend?" I asked her.

"Tasha, it's not that I hate her. It's just that I'm a good judge of people's character, and I never trusted her from the first time that I met her. I will tell you this; just like I don't trust her, I also don't believe that she is going to take rejection well either," she said.

"Kim, all I have to say to that is that she better not come for me if I'm not coming for her. I played nice today, but I promise you that I will not be so nice next time," I said, seriously.

"So how did she take it when you told her the friendship was over?" she asked.

"She didn't understand how her fucking with Lah had anything to do with me not wanting to be her friend anymore. I tried to explain to her that it had to do with being loyal and how I felt that if she could sleep with a married man, what would make mine off limits, but she wasn't getting it."

"I'm just glad that bitch is out of the picture, but be sure to watch your back because, like I said, she's doesn't seem like the type to swallow rejection well. Okay, I'm done being nosey. I have to go and get Will's dinner on the table," she said, laughing again.

"Okay, I will talk to you later, nosey ass," I laughed, ending the call.

~

It's been about a week since my friendship ended with Jasmine, and I don't know if I was being paranoid, but shit has been happening, and it was starting to freak me the fuck out. I went to pick Madison up from school, and when I came out, both of my back tires were flat. Then the other day, I get a call from Children's Hospital, telling me that RJ was brought in from school, and they couldn't give me any information over the phone. Rellz and I rushed to the hospital to only find out that they didn't have our fucking son. I called his school, and they informed me that not only was he in school, but he had been fine all day. Rellz was starting to look at me like I was losing my fucking mind, but I'm not losing my fucking mind. I did get that call.

I didn't want to point any fingers, but I think that Jasmine is behind all the shit that's been happening lately. I finally blocked her on Facebook because all of her subliminal messages that I knew were about me. She had the nerve to post on her wall that, "Bitches worried about who the next bitch's man is fucking but need to worry about who their man is fucking." Now I know for a fact that her message was for me, but I didn't even respond. I just blocked the bitch, and since I blocked her, I have been getting all types of sexual messages from men in my inbox. This bitch was being real petty because I didn't want to be her friend anymore. She better pray she's not the one who's playing games when it comes to my fucking kids because I will kill that simple bitch. I didn't tell Rellz who I thought it was because he would snap her fucking neck - no questions asked.

Chapter Fifteen (Jasmine)

I felt sick to my stomach, watching my ex-friend chilling with her new friends, Chink and Polo, and her fat friend, Kim, who hated me from the first day that she met me. I just knew that she's the one who put all that shit in Tasha's head to stop fucking with me. The Cheesecake Factory used to be our favorite spot, and now she's here with them, having a good time like our friendship never meant anything to her. If she thinks that the flat tire and that fake call from the hospital was bad, she hasn't seen anything yet because I'm just getting started. All those bitches are going to wish that they never tried me.

I no longer had Lah, and Rellz fell back from seeing me out of fear that Tasha was going to find out about us, but I've got something for his ass too. I watched as they all said their goodbyes and went their separate ways. I waited a few minutes after Kim pulled out until I decided to follow her. I didn't know that it was going to take an hour following this bitch home. I knew that I couldn't let her make it inside because I didn't know if her husband was going to be home or not. When she exited her car, I moved fast and was now standing in front of her. The look of fear on her face gave me that extra push that I needed.

"Jasmine, what are you doing here?" she asked, stuttering.

"Don't look so surprised to see me. Weren't you the one who filled Tasha's head with all of the don't trust me bullshit?" I asked her.

She kept looking at her house. I guess she was trying to figure out if should she scream or at least hope that her husband would look out and save her ass, but by the time he even realized that she was home, it would be too late. She went to grab me, but I was ready for her. I had already figured that she would try me being she was a big, fat bitch, and I was petite, but I knew just how to handle her ass. I took the knife that I had in my hand and stabbed her repeatedly in her stomach until she fell to the ground. I stabbed her a few more times in her neck before getting the fuck out of dodge. Tasha should have listened to her fat ass friend, Kim. She was on to something. I laughed to myself as I got in my car and pulled off. Once I made it to the Lincoln Tunnel, I was able to breathe easy again. I had one more stop before picking up my daughter and taking my ass home.

After feeding Ariel and getting her ready for bed, I sat on my couch, bored to death. I no longer had a friend, or any fuck buddies, so a bitch was going crazy, having no one to talk to and no one to fuck. I sent Rellz a text message to give him another chance to change his mind about continuing to be my fuck buddy, but he never responded. I hated to have to do him dirty, but if he thought that he could just break things off because he is scared of his bitch ass wife, he is now on my hit list. Lah changed his number, so I couldn't even hit him up to try and entice him like I used to, but it's all good. I'm going to show each and every last one of them what happens when you fuck me over.

I had decided to make a fake Facebook page so that I could stalk Lah's ass to see what he was up to. I logged on to see if he had accepted me, but he hadn't yet. Frustrated, I shut down the computer and went to pour a glass of wine. I needed to figure out what my next move would be. Both of these motherfuckers are laid up with their wives, and I have nobody. Remember the saying, misery loves company? I'm about to invite a few people to this party. I'll be damned if I'm the only one miserable when I wasn't the only one who was at fault. These fucking women always punish the female but have no problem forgiving their cheating ass men.

~

The next morning, I was up watching the news, waiting for them to report the stabbing of Kim because I needed to make sure that she was dead. I was sure of it, but it's always better to be safe than sorry. As soon as it was confirmed that the bitch was dead, I started to put my next plan into motion. I hated to do it, but it needed to be done because motherfuckers needed to know that I wasn't one to be fucked with.

I sat outside of Rellz's club in Midtown; I wasn't sure if I was going to be able to pull this off because it seemed like people walked the damn street every few minutes. It was already ten on a Wednesday night, and I couldn't understand, for the life of me, why the fuck these people were still out here. *'Date night must be any night of the week,'* I thought as I watched couple after couple, enjoying the light breeze that was blowing. I really didn't need for the streets to be clear, but I just wanted to be careful and not draw attention to myself or be seen by anyone.

I got out of the car, put my hood over my head, and walked toward the back of the club. Tonight wasn't a club night but being the club was located near a few restaurants, you never knew who was lurking. I took the keys to the back door out of my pocket and disarmed the alarm before opening the door. I bet his ass will regret leaving me to lock up the club on so many occasions. A bitch knew that remembering codes and making copies of keys would come in handy somewhere down the line. Call me what you want, but I bet you can never call me a stupid bitch. The club was creepy because it was so dark, but I couldn't turn on any lights. I had to make my way up to Rellz's office using my memory. Once in his office, I handled my business and got the hell out of dodge.

Chapter Sixteen (Tasha)

Rellz and I just got back from attending Kim's funeral. I just didn't believe that she was gone; I just saw her. Polo and Chink attended the funeral with their husbands, and I really appreciated the support from them. They didn't really get to know her as well as I did, but just from those few outings, they knew that she was a good person and would do anything for anyone. Who would want to hurt Kim? Why would someone take her from her husband and her children? She was one of those people that would give you the shirt off her back. This shit hurts me to my core.

"Tash, do you need me to get you anything?" Rellz asked.

"No, I'm okay. I just don't understand who would want to hurt Kim," I cried.

"I don't know, Tash. Her husband said that he heard when she pulled up to the house, but he didn't think to greet her at the door because it's just not something that he ever did. So, he's blaming himself being she was killed right outside of their home," he said.

"He can't blame himself; he had no way of knowing that someone would try to hurt her right outside of their home. They have lived on that same block for five years, so who would have thought that danger was lurking, especially when she was loved by everyone that knew her," I cried, wiping my tears.

"I'm really sorry for your loss, baby, and if you need anything, I'm here for you," he said, hugging me.

I went upstairs to get out of the clothes that I wore to the funeral. I just couldn't stop my tears from falling. She just had the twins six months ago, and she was so happy because she and Will had been trying for two years to conceive. When she found out that she was pregnant, she was so excited. Now, her babies have to grow up without their mother. This shit hurts; it seems like I'm always losing my loved ones. I took a shower, put on my nightclothes, and got into the bed.

Rellz came up a few minutes later with tea and some Tylenol to help me sleep. I woke up the next morning, still in my funk, but I knew that I had to be a mother because life goes on. I called Will to check on him and the kids; he told me that the twins were with Kim's mother until he was able to care for them. I let him know that I was here for him, and if he needed me for anything, to give me a call. I felt so bad for him. His world was turned upside down overnight; Kim was his everything. I still had a slight headache, but I didn't let it stop me from getting breakfast on the table.

Rellz was going to be at the club tonight, so later, he was taking the kids to stay the weekend with my aunt, and Chink and Polo were coming over to keep my company. We were going to have a ladies night sleepover. I really wasn't up to it, but I figured that having company would take my mind off of losing my friend - at least for one night. After breakfast, we all sat in the living room, watching Saturday morning cartoons. I felt a little better after spending time with the kids and Rellz; they always made me feel better whenever I was going through something.

The day went pretty fast, and it was already time for Rellz to drop the kids off to my aunt. I kissed them all goodbye before going to straighten up before Chink and Polo arrived. They told me not to do anything because they were going to bring food and snacks for our sleepover. Chink called to say that they were on their way, and when I ended the call with her, I called my aunt to check on the kids. She said that they were doing well. She had just gotten them washed, and she was putting them to bed. Rellz texted my phone to let me know that he was at the club and to tell me to try and enjoy myself.

Chink and Polo got to my house about ten, and I'm not going to lie, I felt a lot better. They had my ass up in here laughing and enjoying their company. We were watching

Survivor's Remorse, Season One, On Demand, and I loved it. Tichina Arnold and Mike Epps were too damn funny, and that damn gay sister of Cam's was a trip. We was sipping on some Rosé Moscato, which was still one of my favorite drinks, so even if the shit wasn't funny, I was going to be laughing because I was never a big drinker, and I was feeling a little tipsy. Two drinks were my limit, and they were enough to have my ass tipsy and giggling all night. We all jumped at the sound of glass breaking. Polo jumped up and went to look out of the window to see what the hell was going on.

"What the fuck?" I heard her say as she went to open the door.

When Chink and I got to the door, Polo was going off because someone had thrown a brick through the back window of the brand new car that she had just gotten. She was freaking out and using curse words that I didn't think a white girl even knew.

"Who the fuck would do some fucked up shit like this?" I asked, and we all looked at each other with a knowing look.

"I know that bitch, Jasmine, isn't coming for me because that bitch is coming for the wrong one. I will have her whole family wearing black," Polo said.

"Tasha, get the keys to your car. We are going to this bitch's house," Polo said, running back inside to put her sneakers on.

"Polo, we are all in our pajamas. Where the fuck are we going, dressed like this?" I said, causing us all to laugh.

"And I'm not going to lie; my ass is tipsy, and Chink's ass is tipsy too, and you just learned how to drive. I don't feel like dying tonight." I burst out laughing.

"That shit is not funny. Why did that bitch throw a brick through my fucking window? Chink is the one that's dick blocking, and Tasha, your ass pulled your friendship card," Polo said, causing us to all laugh again.

"Don't worry about it, Polo. Since it happened at my house, I will pay for it, but I promise you whatever the cost, it is coming out her ass," I said, meaning every word.

"You don't have to do that; it's not your fault that this bitch threw a fucking brick, and we really don't know that it was her," Polo tried to reason, but who else could it have been?

We went outside with some black garbage bags and tape to seal off the broken window until morning. Polo went to take the brick out of the backseat, and she came out with the brick and a DVD that said, "Play me," on it.

"What the fuck is this shit?" she asked, examining the DVD.

"Only one way to find out." I took it out of her hand.

We went back into the living room. We all looked nervous, but I wanted to see what was on the fucking DVD. I put the DVD into the player and used the remote to press play. It was kind of dark, but I could tell that it was Rellz's office because of the fish tank that he had built into the wall. All we could see at first were two silhouettes who were clearly fucking by all of the moaning that the female was doing. When they changed positions, the light from the fish tank showed a clear picture of Rellz bending Jasmine over the desk and fucking the shit out of her.

I felt my stomach churn, making me feel as if I had to throw up. I ran upstairs to the bathroom, just making it to the toilet. I felt like I was choking off of my own vomit because it wasn't easy throwing up and crying at the same time. Chink and Polo were now in the bathroom with me. Chink was pulling my hair out of my face, and Polo was rubbing my back. I appreciated the gesture, but I just wanted to be left alone. How could I be so fucking stupid and not know that this bitch was fucking my husband? All types of things were going through my head, like if she started fucking him after I broke off the friendship or before. To be honest, it really didn't matter. This bitch had crossed the fucking line, and she was going to get dealt with.

My tears disappeared and were now replaced with anger as I went into my closet and pulled out some jeans and a sweatshirt. I put my sneakers on, and I was ready to go. I didn't even realize that Chink and Polo were now fully dressed as I grabbed my car keys before Polo took them from me. Once in the car, she asked me where we were going, and I told her to take me to Rellz's club.

Chapter Seventeen (Chink)

We got to the club, and Tasha barged through security with us following suit. She took two steps at a time, trying to reach Rellz's office. I didn't know what was going to happen at this point, but I was going to have her back. These sorry ass men are just straight fucking nasty. Is the pussy that fucking good? Tasha reached Rellz's office, and when she noticed that he wasn't in there, she went into a fit of rage as she grabbed whatever was in her reach. I saw a side of her that I didn't know she had in her as she started fucking his office up. All of the papers and everything else that was on his desk, she swept it off onto the floor. She picked up the office chair and swung it into the built-in fish tank. Glass, water, and fish were everywhere. I didn't think that an office chair would be able to break the glass, but it did.

Polo and I backed up out of the office, pulling her with us, because we were about to get locked up, fucking with her ass. Security was now coming up the stairs to try and get her to calm down, and she cursed them out, telling them to not fucking touch her. I have never seen someone display that much rage and not be tired; I thought that Polo was a beast, but Tasha had taken that title. She went through the club like a tornado, looking for Rellz, but it was clear that he wasn't at the club like he said he was. She did so much damage to the club that once she went and knocked bottles of liquor down, one of the bouncers had had enough as he grabbed her and escorted her out of the club.

"Take me to that bitch, Jasmine's, house, right fucking now!" she yelled, breathing fast and looking like a crazy woman.

"Tasha, maybe it's not a good idea to go to her house. I don't want you getting arrested," I tried to reason.

"Well, if you're not going to take me, give me the keys to my car, and I will drive myself there," she said.

"I'm not going to let you get behind the wheel like this. Give me the address, and I'll take you," Polo said. I really didn't agree, but I was riding out with them.

It took us about thirty minutes to get to Jasmine's house, and when we pulled up, Rellz's fucking car was in her driveway. His ass had to be the stupidest motherfucker in the world; I knew that he was fucking because I knew that somebody from the club had to try and reach out to his ass to tell him they had to shut the club down because of his crazy ass wife.

Tasha jumped out of the car and ran up on the porch. She started banging on the door, yelling for Rellz to bring his ass out of the house. After ten minutes of banging and kicking on the door, his punk ass still hadn't come out of the house, and she lost it. She picked up a brick, that she got from the neighbor's yard, and started destroying both of their cars. We tried to reason with her that someone was going to call the cops, and we needed to leave, but she wasn't trying to hear me as she picked up another brick, breaking the window to the first floor of the house.

Just as she was going to try and climb through the window, the front door opened, and Rellz came out onto the porch. She ran up on him, swinging wildly and calling him all kinds of names. I went to turn around to tell Polo that this was enough, and we needed to get her because she was going to end up going to jail, but Polo was already running past them into the house.

"Polo, NOOOOO!" I yelled.

I ran in behind Polo, and she was fucking Jasmine up. I didn't know if I should pull her off of the girl or not, but seeing that this bitch was still laughing like shit was funny, I joined in on beating that ass. At this point, all I could think of was this bitch riding my man's dick as I kicked her in every fucking spot that Polo wasn't abusing. As soon as I went to lift my foot to stomp her in her fucking face, my foot stopped in mid-air as I heard an officer telling us to freeze and to move away from her.

Needless to say, Tasha, Polo, and I were all placed in handcuffs, and that bitch was escorted to the fucking hospital. Once in the back of the police car, Tasha looked at Polo and I, and we all burst out laughing. No, it wasn't funny that we were being arrested, but we laughed to keep from crying. Rellz was arrested too, but they put him into another patrol car. Well, I didn't know if he was being arrested or if he was just being taken down for questioning.

Lah was going to kick my ass for being out here fighting like a fucking teenager, but I didn't care. I would do it all over again if given the chance. My fucking nails were broke the fuck up. I looked over at Tasha, and she was now silently crying. I knew this shit hurt her to find his stinking, cheating ass at the bitch's house. It made me start to wonder if Lah was still fucking her behind my back too; I don't know what that bitch did to these niggas, but both of them had to be in a pussy whipped coma.

"Don't cry, Tasha. He's not even worth your tears right now." I tried to comfort her.

"I know, but I can't help it. I'm so fucking hurt right now, and if I had a gun, I would have shot his dumb ass in the fucking dick," she said seriously.

"Polo, you good?" I asked her because she was quiet.

"I'm good; with the way I tried to kill that bitch, you would have thought she fucked my man too," she whispered.

"Shit; I wouldn't put it past that hoe ass bitch. She's fucking nasty. How you fucking both of them, knowing they family?" Tasha asked.

Once we got to the police station, they put all three of us in the same cell. I was just happy to get those cuffs off of my hands. If Polo and Tasha weren't here, I probably would have been scared to death, being in a jail cell.

"So, are you calling Liem to let him know what happened, or do you want me to call Lah?" I asked Polo.

"It doesn't matter; either way we fucked," she said.

"I'm sorry. It's my fault that we're even in here," Tasha apologized.

"I told you that we had your back; we're in this shit together," I told her.

Once we were processed, the officer let me use the phone to make a call. I started to call my aunt, but I decided against it and just called Lah. I told him that we were down at the 113th precinct, but I didn't think that we qualified for a desk appearance. I got off of the phone with him, feeling a little better because he sounded more concerned than upset with me. He said that he was going to call Liem and let him know what was going on. He said that they would be there so not to worry. Tasha called her brother, and he said that he would be there as well. I wasn't proud of being fingerprinted and being in the system, but I was glad that I didn't work for anyone but myself because this would not have been a good look.

We sat in that cell, joking and trying to make the time pass quickly, but all jokes came to a cease once we made it to central booking. It was really a nightmare, and I was ready to go home. Tasha was being charged with vandalism, and Polo and I were being charged with assault and battery. At arraignment, we were all released on recognizance – meaning we were basically released without bail. I felt bad once I saw that Liem and Lah had to bring the children with them. Tasha introduced us to her brother, Kane, before we all went our separate ways. I didn't know what was going to happen once they got home, but I knew that I was going to have to answer a million and one questions, and I would be chastised for acting as if I wasn't a mother and wife.

Chapter Eighteen (Rellz)

I didn't know if I should wait around once I was released from the police station or just go to the house while Tasha was detained and get some of my belongings. I fucked up, and I'm pissed at myself. When Lah got caught up, I said that I wasn't going to fuck with Jasmine anymore, but somehow, I ended up back in her bed. I don't know how Tasha knew that I was at her house, and if I wasn't dick deep in Jasmine's ass, I would have gotten the call that Tasha was up at the club, causing havoc. Knowing Tasha, my club was going to be shut down for renovations because when she blacks out, it's a wrap.

I have this big ass knot on the side of my head to prove it and a fucked up ride to further prove my point. I decided to go to the house, and when I pulled up, I noticed that Polo's car was in my yard, fucked up as well. I went inside and saw the video that I made with me fucking Jasmine in my office, frozen on the screen. I didn't even need to press play because I already knew that it was, in fact, my DVD from my office. That bitch had set me up, and I fell for the shit. How the fuck had I let this bitch catch me slipping for some fucking pussy?

I should of known that something was up when she called me tonight, telling me how much she missed me and all the things that she wanted to do with my dick. Being Tasha was having a sleepover, and the club was running smoothly, I decided to go and get my dick wet, not knowing that the bitch was setting me up the whole time. To think that I was feeling sorry for the bitch getting jumped on by Polo and Chink, when she set this shit up. Somebody should have told her that she fucked with the wrong nigga. I grabbed a few things, locked the front door, and headed to the club before going to stay at a hotel for the night.

I could have stayed with Turk, but when I called to tell him what happened, he was entertaining yet another female. I thought that after becoming a father, he would have settled down, but it didn't last long. His baby momma jumped ship because he refused to keep it in his pants, so she was now living in Canada with her mother. He takes care of his child and visits her, but it really hurt him that she left with his child. His ass had the nerve to say that he would never give his heart to another woman when he was the reason she left.

I was bad, but I wasn't as bad as Turk. I really loved my wife, but sometimes the dog in me comes out to play, but I always take my ass home. I'm not going to lie; there was something about Jasmine that had me jumping through hoops for her ass; I can't say that I had fallen in love with her, but I was definitely feeling her. She had me still fucking with her ass once I found out that she was messing with Lah. I have to admit, she had my ass whipped on some pussy.

When I got to the club, I rubbed my temples before opening up the door because I already knew that I wasn't going to like what I was going to see on the other side of the door. The first thing that I saw was broken liquor bottles all over the floor, and the stench of all of the different liquors were in the air. I was fucking livid when I saw my office. How in the fuck did all of the security, that I had on payroll, let her do this shit? Yes, she's the wife, but they could have carried her ass up out of here. My phone rang, and I wasn't even going to answer it, but when I saw that it was Kane, I picked up.

"What's up, Kane?" I asked.

"Yo, what the fuck happened?" I knew he was asking because Tasha wouldn't tell him the whole story.

"Man, this bitch, Jasmine, sent Tasha a DVD of us fucking, and Tasha came to my club, looking for my ass. I wasn't at the club, so she fucked shit up there before coming to Jasmine's house with her new friends and tearing shit up over there. She hit me in my fucking head with a fucking brick, and her girls fucked Jasmine up. Someone called the cops, and they came and arrested all three of them. They took me to the police station, wanting me to press charges, but I told those nigga that I didn't want to press charges. They were pissed off, but I didn't give a fuck. She's still my fucking wife, and it was my fault that she was wilding out in the first place," I explained.

"Well, I went to court, and she didn't get no bond. She's home, and I took her to pick up the kids yesterday. She doesn't want anything to do with your ass right now, so just give her some space because I don't need her to get re-arrested for busting you in your head again. Also, Jasmine is going to have to fall back too as far as pressing charges. It's not so much Tasha, but her friends charges are pretty fucking serious," he said, but I didn't know if I wanted to even speak to this bitch because I didn't know if I would be able to talk to her without catching my own fucking case.

I wanted to shut that bitch up permanently, but I couldn't kill the mother of my child. Yes, Ariel belonged to me. Jasmine isn't playing fair, and I know that her next move is going to be to threaten to tell Tasha about the baby being mine. Jasmine and I have been fucking around since the second week that she became friends with Tasha; it was supposed to be a hit it and quit it type of situation, but it became much more with her having my child. I fucked up, having a child outside of my marriage, but it's done, and there is nothing that I can do to change that right now. I tried to talk Jasmine into not having the baby, but she wasn't trying to hear me, so my fucking hands were tied at that point. My whole world is fucked up right now, and I don't even know if I still have a marriage because getting caught with my pants down with her friend isn't something that she's going to be willing to forgive so easily.

I made a call to make sure that my club would be up and running by next weekend, or I was going to have somebody's fucking head. These motherfuckers shouldn't have left this shit sitting like this for no two fucking days. The floor on the first level had to be pulled up because the liquor soaked through the floor; if had they taken care of it when it happened, it probably could have been saved.

I called Tasha's phone, but she sent me straight to voicemail. I really didn't expect her to answer; I just wanted to leave her a voicemail to let her know that I loved her and to tell her that I was sorry. Tasha is stuck on this loyalty and respect thing hard. She has forgiven me time after time, but I don't think that she is going to be able to forgive me this time.

Chapter Nineteen (Chink)

My punishment for getting locked up wasn't as bad as I thought it would be. I just knew that Lah was going to go in and give me the you're a mother speech, but all he really stressed was that we could have really hurt her, and the consequences would have been a lot worse. Jasmine decided not to cooperate with the D.A. for whatever reason. I just hoped that she was going to fall back and leave us the fuck alone.

Tasha hadn't allowed Rellz back home, and I don't think that she is going to take him back. She said that she was really hurting because this wasn't the first time that he had cheated on her, so after taking him back so many times, with him promising never to cheat again, he went and cheated on her with her best friend. He comes and gets the kids on Saturday, keeps them for the entire day, and then brings them back when it's time for him to go to work at the club. Lah told me that Rellz was staying at a hotel, so I let Tasha know that I didn't think that he was still seeing the bitch.

Polo and I have been checking up on her because she has really been in a funk. I tried to give her the same advice that she gave me, but she wasn't trying to hear me. She said that it was different because Lah had fallen victim one time, but Rellz has fallen victim too many times. She said that she was fed up with taking him back only for him to fuck her over again and again. I understood how she felt, so I just left it alone and decided to just continue to be a friend.

I went upstairs to get LJ ready to take his bath so that he could be put to bed. I just wanted to get him down, take a shower, and get ready for ratchet television. When I came out of the bathroom, Lah was sitting on the bed, waiting on me. I sighed loudly because I didn't want to miss my show. Even though I was recording it, I didn't get the same feeling when I watched it later.

"Hey, babe. Can we talk?" he asked me.

"What is it, Lah?" I asked, not hiding that him being in my space irritated me.

"I want to talk about us," he said, and I knew that I wasn't going to have a choice but to watch the recording.

"What about us, Lah?"

"I know that I told you that I was sorry, but I don't think that you understand how sorry," he began.

"And why don't you think that I understand how sorry you are?"

"Well, you gave me another chance, but I just feel like we haven't moved forward, and I'm not talking about sex. Any affection or conversation that you do give me just seems strained," he continued.

"Well, what do you expect from me? This shit isn't going to be fixed overnight; I'm still hurting. Yes, I took you back because I love you, but that doesn't mean that shit is going to go back to being normal right away. It's easy to lose trust but hard getting it back, so that's what I'm struggling with right now."

"I understand that, Chink, but if you're not letting me back in one hundred percent, how am I supposed to prove to you that I love my family, and I'm willing to do whatever it takes to earn that trust back?"

"I'm trying to let you back in, but like I said, it's going to take time to get back to where we were, Lah. You cheated on me and looked me in my face and lied. If you want this then you're going to have to be patient and just continue to prove to me that you want your family."

"Well, can I at least sleep in our bed again as husband and wife? I know I'm still in the doghouse; I promise I'm not going to try anything," he said.

I just smiled at his ass because I knew that if I let his ass back in my bed, he wouldn't be able to restrain himself, and honestly, I didn't know if I wanted him to. I just wished that he could have kept it in his pants because I don't like what has become of our relationship, and I miss being in his arms. I know that if I let him off the hook too soon, I'm going to look stupid, but the distance is killing me, and him looking and smelling good only makes it harder to keep pushing him away.

"So, can I take a shower and come and get in bed and watch ratchet television with you?" he asked.

"Since when do you watch ratchet television?" I asked, not answering his question.

"Since I'm trying to show you that I will do whatever it takes to prove to you that, from now on, it will be about you, my wife. I promise," he answered. He was making my pussy wet, which wasn't good because, if he was going to be in the bed with me, I couldn't use my G-spot Dildo to get me off.

"Lah, go and take a shower, and I will be waiting for you with the remote ready to press play," I said, smiling because I knew that he wasn't going to sit through Love & Hip Hop.

"I know that you don't believe me, but I can show you better than I can tell you," he said before going into the bathroom.

Needless to say, he kept his word and watched television with me until we both dozed off last night. I was impressed because I could never get him to watch. It was a little annoying that I had to answer his questions. He was like who's that, why'd she say that, but I appreciated his company. Before I left for work this morning, I had to go into the bathroom and get myself off because that man had me hot and bothered all night. I told him that I didn't want him to touch me, but if he had touched me, I would have given him the goods. When he reached over and spooned me last night, I felt his hard on, and my shit started dripping. I was just going to take the dick, but I couldn't make the first move after I said that he was still in the doghouse.

I was removing the rollers from my client's hair when I heard my cellphone ringing. I excused myself to take the call.

"Hello?" I said, answering the call.

"Hello; can I speak with Chasity Morales?" the caller asked.

"This is she; who's calling?"

"This is Susan Miles. I'm a nurse at Lincoln Hospital. We have your aunt, Shirley Montgomery, here, and I need for you to get here as soon as possible."

"What happened?" I asked, in a panic.

"Ms. Morales, I'm not at liberty to give any more information over the phone, due to hospital policy," she replied, pissing me off.

I just hung up the phone and apologized to my client before running out of the shop. I tried to slow down my breathing and calm my nerves a little because the last thing I needed was to have an accident when I was trying to get to the hospital to see about my aunt. I called Lah to let him know to pick up LJ after he got off of work and to meet me at the hospital. He asked me question after question, but I had no answers for him. I pulled up to the hospital, parked the car, and went inside to find out what was going on with my aunt.

"Hello. I got a call from a nurse telling me that my aunt was here," I informed the security guard.

He spoke into his radio and informed me that someone would be out to speak to me. My nerves were shot from not knowing what had happened to my aunt. Just as I was about to call my Aunt Sherry to let her know that I was at the hospital, I heard someone ask for the family of Shirley Montgomery.

"I'm Shirley Montgomery's niece," I said.

"Yes, Ms. Morales. I spoke with you on the phone. Your aunt was brought into the hospital this morning with a head injury, which caused her to slip into a coma."

"How did she get a head injury?" I asked her.

"The only information that we have was from her aide that came in with the emergency unit. She stated that your aunt fell down the steps this morning, and when she got to her, she was unresponsive. The aide called 911."

"My aunt doesn't have an aide. She lives alone since my uncle passed away last year, and she's perfectly healthy. She isn't in need of an aide," I said, confused.

She looked at the chart that she was holding in her hand for a few minutes too long, if you asked me. She looked up at me with a stupid look on her face.

"Ms. Morales, the aide's name isn't in the report. It just says that the aide was the one who made the call and rode with your aunt in the ambulance. She left the hospital after she gave Ms. Montgomery's next of kin information," she explained.

"So, the aide was a female?" I asked her.

"Yes, the aide was a woman," she replied.

"Did she leave her agency's name and number or even her number?" I asked, still really confused.

"No, we don't have any information on the woman that came in with your aunt." She spoke like she was getting frustrated with my line of questioning.

I wanted to see my aunt, but there was nothing that I could do for her right now. My concern was whether or not it was Jasmine who hurt her. My aunt didn't have an aide to care for her, and I thought that the whole riding to the hospital with my aunt was that crazy bitch's way of letting us know that it was her. She's taking this shit too far, and from here on out, it's murder she wrote. Mark my words. If my fucking aunt needed an aide, she wouldn't have been able to care for my son whenever we took him to her, which was often.

Chapter Twenty (Lah)

It's been two weeks since Chink's aunt was hospitalized, and there was still no change in her condition. Chink's Aunt Sherry and her husband were here from Texas, so I finally got her to take one day off from going to the hospital because it was really taking a toll on her. Chink was hell bent that Jasmine was at fault for what happened to her aunt. She's been stressing it, and her partner in crime wasn't making it any better, talking about revenge when they really didn't have any proof. Usually I would just handle it, but I didn't believe that Jasmine would go this far by hurting an innocent person. I called up Rellz and spoke to him to get his take on it, and he felt the same way that I feel. Chink's mind was made up about her being the culprit, and she wasn't going to stop until Jasmine paid for what she did to her aunt.

LJ was sleeping, and Chink was in bed, lying down. I told her that I was going out for a few, and I promised that I wouldn't be gone for any longer than half an hour. I knew that I shouldn't even be thinking about going near Jasmine's ass, but I needed to go and talk to her to make sure that she had nothing to do with what happened to Chink's aunt. I pulled up to her house at the same time that my cuz was pulling up. I couldn't help but wonder if he was showing up to her house after every time that I left her house.

"Hey, cuz. What are you doing here?" I asked him.

"I just had to come and make sure that this bitch wasn't taking personal hits because I can't have this bitch coming at my family next," he said.

"That's the reason I'm here too. Chink really believes that Jasmine is behind this shit, and to keep it funky, cuz, if she did this, she has already came after your family," I said.

"Right," he agreed as we walked up her walkway with him knocking on the door.

After ten minutes with still no answer, he went around back and came back with the key to the front door. The bitch never told me where the spare key was, so she had to be kicking it with him for a minute. We walked inside, and the only thing that was in the living room was the couch. He went upstairs while I looked around the rest of the house. It didn't take a scientist to know that this bitch was ghost.

"Yo, cuz, this bitch moved out," he said, looking pissed off. "So maybe the bitch did have something to do with Chink's aunt being hurt. What other reason would she have to run and take my fucking daughter with her?"

"Your daughter?" I asked.

"Yeah, my daughter. That's the only reason that bitch is still breathing after sending that fucking tape to my wife," he said, punching the wall.

I didn't know what to say to him, but if he was planning on trying to get back with his wife, his ass better tell her because if she finds this out from Jasmine, who is clearly being messy right now, it's going to mess up any chance that he has of getting her back. I didn't say anything to him about talking to his wife about having a daughter with Jasmine, but I did tell him that we should hook up on the weekend so that we could try to figure out how we were going to go about finding where she ran off to. He wanted to go to a couple of spots tonight, but I told him that I promised Chink that I was only going to be gone for no longer than a half an hour, and I wasn't trying to go back in the doghouse.

I couldn't believe that I let my dick get me hooked up with some crazy bitch that's stuck on revenge because she can no longer have the dick. I mean India was crazy, but she wasn't going after my family, trying to hurt them, because I didn't want to fuck with her anymore. When I got back to the house, Chink was sitting on the couch, watching television. She gave me that I told you so look which let me know that Liem already told Polo about Jasmine being missing. I told him not to say anything to Polo until I talked to Chink. His ass better start acting like he wears the fucking pants in that relationship.

"I told you that she had something to do with my aunt being hurt. Had you let me go after that bitch the day that it happened, she wouldn't have had time to go missing," she said, pissed off.

"Babe, I just found it hard to believe that she would go after your aunt to hurt her just because you're the reason I wasn't fucking with her anymore," I said, not knowing what else to say.

"I should have just went with my gut and ran up on that bitch and not worried about who believed she did it or not," she responded.

"Babe, Rellz is going to try and find her. He said that he knows a couple of places where she might be hiding out, so don't worry. We've got this," I said.

I didn't know if I should tell her that Rellz was the father of Jasmine's daughter and that he knew a lot more about her than we did, but I was afraid that if I told her that to give her hope that we would find her, she would tell Tasha before Rellz got the chance to. I would hate for her to come at another one of our family members again, so I really hope that he knew where to find her ass.

I went to sit next to Chink on the couch because she was clearly upset. I pulled her into my arms in an attempt to calm her down. Her cellphone rang, so I released her so that she could take the call. I went into the kitchen to get a bottle of water because I needed to take a Tylenol; my head was banging from all of the stress that I had been feeling lately. I walked back into the living room, and Chink said that her Aunt Sherry called to tell her that her Aunt Shirley woke up. She wanted to rush to the hospital, but I told her to get some rest, and we would go up to the hospital tomorrow because visiting hours were over for the night, and they weren't going to let her see her aunt anyway.

I told her to go up, take a shower, and get into bed and that I would be right behind her. I needed to call Rellz to let him know that I didn't do well with stress, and we needed to find Jasmine because as long as Chink was stressed, I was going to continue to stress. He said that he was going to go to the babysitter that Jasmine uses sometimes, who lives in Queensbridge, to see if she was hiding out there. I let him know that Chink's aunt was awake, so after dropping LJ off to my pops and his wife, we would be up at the hospital and for him to make sure that he gives me a call if he finds out anything.

Chapter Twenty-One (Tasha)

I was missing Rellz like crazy, but I refused to take his ass back. Everything bothered me, including these damn kids. I needed a break because my mental was slowly but surely fading away, and I didn't want to take it out on the kids. Chink told me to come to her house and let her help with the kids for a little while; I really didn't want to impose, but I really needed to take her up on her offer because I was losing it. RJ was just being difficult today, and even Madison was giving me a hard time. If it weren't for the help of the twins, both of their asses would have been buried some damn where. I knew that it had a lot to do with them missing Rellz, but I just couldn't take him back right now, not even for the kids.

Once the kids were ready to go, I grabbed the keys to the mini-van so that we could head out. When I opened the screen door, I almost knocked something off the porch. I told the kids to step back so that I could investigate what the hell was blocking the door. I couldn't believe that this crazy bitch left her fucking baby on my porch, sitting in her car seat, wrapped in a blanket. I picked up the car seat and headed back inside, telling the kids to have a seat for a second. RJ started to whine because, once he has his jacket on, he's ready to go. I opened up the blanket to make sure that Ariel was okay. I couldn't believe that this crazy ass girl had a fucking note safety pinned to Ariel's sweater.

I took the pin loose and was contemplating if I really wanted to read the note. In all honesty, what could possibly be the reason this bitch would leave her fucking baby on my porch? We weren't friends anymore, so she shouldn't have even thought that she had a reason to come anywhere near my fucking house. Before I called the police to let them know that this crazy bitch had left her baby on my porch, I decided to just read the note.

So you decided to side with these bitches, come to my house and tear shit up, and allow them to harm me for a man that you knew was fucking cheating on you. No, you didn't know that he was cheating on you with me, but you still knew that he was cheating. I just want to let you know that you hurt me by picking those two bitches, that you knew for a good two days, over me, who you have known longer. We could have worked this out because, to be honest with you, I don't want your man like that; it was just sex for me. We both know that you're going to take him back, so since you're already playing house with his son, that doesn't belong to you, you may as well take care of his daughter, too. I wasn't going to come for you had you not played me for a fucking bitch and her husband that had nothing to do with you. So, all I have left to say to you is, treat my baby just like you treat RJ, and don't worry, it won't be for long because your days are numbered. I'M COMING FOR YOU AND ALL THOSE BITCHES!!!

Oh, before I forget, if you're thinking about going to the police about me leaving my baby on your doorstep, don't. I left her with her father, so she wasn't abandoned; she was just left to spend some quality time with her daddy. See you soon, bitch...

I just stood still, with the letter in my hand, not knowing what to do or even think at this point. I never knew that this bitch had mental issues. Why the fuck did she feel the need to do me dirty? She's the bitch that slept with someone's husband behind her back, and on top of that, she slept with my husband behind my back also, so she's mad at me for what? Not only was she going behind my back, creeping with my husband, she had a fucking baby with him, so if she wanted to threaten me that she was coming for me, she better pray that she got me before I got her ass.

I called Chink and let her know what this crazy bitch did, and she said that she was going to have Lah hit Rellz up, and she was on her way. I didn't really want to see Rellz, but if this was his seed, he needed to come and get the little bitch. I wasn't going to take out my frustrations on the baby because,

146

at the end of the day, she had nothing to do with her mother being a crazy bitch or her father being a cheating dog. I picked her up, and the crazy bitch had her sitting on a copy of her birth certificate along with another note stating that, if I didn't believe that she was Rellz's, she decided to add the proof, along with the DNA results. All I could do was fucking laugh at this crazy bitch to keep from crying out in anger.

She had me wanting to punch a fucking wall. I swear on everything I love, I'm emptying a clip in that bitch when I find her. I told the twins to help me get the kids out of their jackets, and as soon as she took RJ's jacket off, he went into a screaming fit. I told Saniyah to come into the kitchen and get a cookie for him, just so he could shut the hell up. While I was in the kitchen, I made Ariel a bottle. To think this bitch asked me to be the godmother of a baby that belonged to my fucking husband made me sick to my stomach. Those weekends that I agreed to keep Ariel were probably the weekends they were using to hook up.

Chink called my phone, letting me know that she was out front, because I refused to open the door. I told her to call me when she was outside, just in case it was that crazy bitch on my doorstep again with one of her fucking games. I let Chink and Lah in and made sure to lock the door behind them. I really wanted Chink to come by herself because I was already embarrassed about this whole situation, but I knew that she brought him with her in case I decided to go Rambo on Rellz's ass.

"Lah spoke to Rellz, and he said that he was on his way," Chink informed me. "Polo and Liem are on the way too."

I know that she could tell that I was trying to be strong and not show emotion, but to be honest, I didn't know how much longer it would be before I snapped. I asked her to keep the baby for me while I went upstairs to get the other children situated. Chink stopped by McDonald's and got them something to eat; I usually don't let them eat in their rooms, but I didn't need them downstairs while the grown-ups were talking. I thought about that stink bitch having the nerves to say that I'm playing house with Rellz's fucking son; RJ may be his son, but that's still my fucking nephew. I felt my anger rising as I heard Rellz's voice downstairs. I took a deep breath, trying to calm my nerves.

"Are you going to be okay? I just came upstairs to let you know that Polo and Liem are here. Rellz is downstairs too," Chink said as she entered my room.

"Chink, I feel like I'm about to lose it. I really don't want to see him right now because I'm afraid of what I'm going to do to his ass. A fucking baby that he had me thinking I was being a godmother to when I was really being a fucking stepmother," I cried as the tears that I tried so hard to fight released down my face.

"This shit is fucked up on so many levels, and I don't understand why men never realize that their actions always end up hurting the people that they claim to love," she said, rubbing my back.

"Just the thought that he was never going to tell me, hurts me more than anything. Had she not been sleeping with Lah and got caught, none of the shit would have came out, and he would have had me continuing to play the fool for both of their asses."

"I know how you feel, but we need to go downstairs and put our heads together to see how we're going to go about finding this bitch. My aunt told me that she was exiting her bathroom, and on her way downstairs to make her breakfast, when a female that fits Jasmine's description, besides the glasses that my aunt said she was wearing, came up behind her and pushed her down the stairs. I didn't even tell her that I knew who did this to her because that ass is mine," she said, seriously.

Chapter Twenty-Two (Rellz)

I just got to the house, and I'm not going to lie, I had been shitting bricks since I got the call from Lah. This bitch, Jasmine, took this shit too far by dropping off my daughter and telling Tasha before I got the chance to tell her. At this point, I didn't give a fuck if she was the mother of my daughter anymore; she's as good as dead. I took a deep breath before getting out of my truck and walking up to the house. I used my key to enter the house, and I walked into the living room where Lah, Polo, and Liem were sitting. Polo rolled her eyes at me as she handed me Ariel; I couldn't even be mad at her because I fucked up. They were really riding for Tasha; Polo was straight gangsta as she sat there, giving me that face that said I want to fuck you up. I diverted my eyes as I walked over to put Ariel in her car seat so that I could go upstairs to say hi to the kids. Just as I was about to go upstairs, Tasha was coming downstairs behind Chink, so I decided to hold off on speaking to the kids. I really didn't want to discuss the situation in front of everybody because this was between her and me. I knew that she wasn't going to want to speak to me, but I decided to give it a shot anyway.

"Tash, can I speak to you alone in the kitchen please?" I asked her.

"Rellz, I don't want to talk to you about anything right now other than how the fuck we are going to get at this bitch," she said.

"Yes, because that bitch had to have a death wish when she thought it would be okay to touch my sis's fucking aunt," Polo added.

"Like I told Lah, I know of a few places that she might be hiding out at, but I haven't had the chance to explore all of the places. I ran up in her friend's crib out in Queensbridge, but she wasn't there. She has this dude that she was fucking with in Far Rockaway so that was going to be my next stop before I got the call from Lah," I said.

"So, what were you doing, stalking the bitch? How the fuck do you know where a dude she was fucking with lays his head?" Tasha asked.

"Look, Tash. Taking shots isn't going to get us anywhere. You didn't want to excuse yourself and talk to me about the shit, so don't go there. We're just trying to find the bitch," I spat, pissed at her for coming at me in front of everybody.

Just as we were starting to continue talking about what the next move would be, the baby starting crying, so I picked her up. Tasha rolled her eyes and left out of the room, with Chink and Polo going behind her. I laid her on her blanket on the couch so that I could change her pamper. She was still crying after I changed her, so I figured that she must have been hungry. I went into the kitchen to ask Tasha if she gave Ariel a bottle, and she went off.

"So, you think that I wouldn't feed an innocent baby behind the fact that you can't keep your dick in your pants?" she yelled.

"Tash, I was only asking because she's crying, and I wanted to know when the last time she had a bottle was before I give her another one," I said, really getting pissed off. I understand I fucked up, but this shit is unnecessary right now.

"Well, she had a bottle about an hour ago, but she didn't drink the whole bottle, so she's probably ready for the rest of it," she said, taking Ariel out of my arms.

I shook my head and went back into the living room with Lah and Liem because Tasha was fucking my head up right now. I'm so fucking pissed that Jasmine did this bullshit, and the more upset that Tasha got, the more I wanted the bitch dead.

"We need to find Jasmine and deal with her ass because Tasha isn't going to give me the time of day until she is dealt with," I said to Lah.

"Sitting here talking about it isn't going to find this bitch. Let's go to dude's crib that you said stay out in Far

Rockaway and see if we can catch this bitch slipping," Lah suggested, and I agreed.

"Tash, we're going to ride out to see if we can find this bitch because sitting here isn't going to find her," I said.

"If you find that bitch, you already know what to do," she said, and I knew exactly what she was requesting. She wanted to be there when we dead the bitch.

I made sure to strap up before riding out. I know Tasha wanted to be there to watch me dead the bitch, but it wasn't going to happen. I was killing this bitch on site. We pulled up outside of the nigga's crib. Lah knocked on the door, and when the nigga answered the door, we violated and pushed up in that bitch.

"Yo, what the fuck you niggas want?" he asked, trying to sound tough, but the look on his face said something different.

"Where's that bitch, Jasmine?" I asked, getting in his face.

"I know you're not still fucking with that bitch?" some chick, that I didn't even notice when we came in the door, said.

"I don't know where the fuck that bitch is; the last time I saw the bitch, she was busting out my wife's car windows," he said.

"Yes, and when I catch up with that bitch, I'm going to bust her fucking head open," his wife said.

Another fucking dead end. I was getting pissed off because I needed to catch up with this bitch sooner than later. We left up out of his crib, offering no apologies for running up in his shit, because I didn't like the nigga to begin with. I sat in my car and decided to see if the bitch would pick up the phone, but the shit was disconnected. I hit the steering wheel with so much force that I thought I broke the shit as the horn blared loudly.

"Cuz, calm down. We're going to find this bitch. She told me that she has no family here, so she will show up soon. It's time to have our wives start calling hotels to see if we can get a hit on one that the bitch might be staying at," Lah said.

"I'm sitting here, shaking my fucking head at you niggas. Not only did the two of you get caught fucking the same bitch, but ya'll got caught up fucking a crazy bitch. Now, this bitch is causing havoc because she can't have the dick anymore. If you motherfuckers swinging the dick like that, causing a bitch to lose her fucking mind, I advise both of you to keep that shit in your fucking pants from now on," Liem said, laughing and causing me and Lah to laugh, even though the shit was true but not funny.

When we got back to the house, all of the kids were down, including Ariel. I didn't know if Tasha was going to let me stay, but I guess I would find out once everyone left. She hadn't spoken two words to me since we had been back, and I wasn't going to push her. Lah and Chink stayed for about another half an hour before calling it a night; I tried to get them to stay as long as possible. Yes, I was acting like a punk because I wasn't ready for the conversation that I knew I would have to have once they left to go home.

I walked them out and made sure that the crazy bitch wasn't lurking with another one of her fucking games that she was playing. I locked the door and made sure shit was secure before going back into the living room to join Tasha on the couch. I didn't know what to say or how to even start up a conversation without it leading into an argument. I fucked up, but I really didn't want to argue; I just wanted to try and offer her an apology to see where we stood as husband and wife. As soon as I opened my mouth to talk to her, she let me know that she didn't want to talk tonight, but she did allow me to stay the night with the baby.

As much as I wanted to see if we could resolve this tonight, to at least come to some type of agreement to where I stood in our relationship, I let it go, at least for tonight. I went upstairs to check on the kids before crashing on the couch. I could have stayed in the guest bedroom, but I didn't want to be upstairs if it wasn't going to be me in the bed with my wife. I finally fell asleep but was woken up out of my sleep because I heard banging on the front door. At first I thought that I was dreaming, but the banging started again. I opened the door, and the NYPD was knocking on the door. I opened the screen door to see what the hell they wanted.

"What can I do for you, officer?" I asked, just knowing that I wasn't going to like the bullshit that was going to come out of his mouth.

"Are you Rellz Jackson?" he asked.

"Yes, I'm Rellz Jackson. Again, what can I do for you?" I asked him.

"Do you have Ariel Jackson in the home?" he continued.

"Yes, I have my daughter here with me. What's the problem?"

"We received a report that you never returned the baby from a weekend visit to her mom," he said.

"I didn't have a weekend visit. Her crazy fucking mother left her on the fucking front porch, and I haven't heard from her," I argued.

"I'm going to need you to calm down. Whether the mother left the baby on the doorstep or not, she has paperwork showing that she has sole custody of the child.

I'm going to need for you to retrieve the child, and any issues that you may have as far as custody or visitation, I suggest that you take them up in family court," he stated.

I wasn't trying to get arrested, but I knew that something was off about these fucking police officers. I wasn't questioning that they were, in fact, police officers, but I thought that the one that was going hard was probably fucking Jasmine. I told the officer to give me a few minutes while I got the baby.

I went upstairs and shook Tasha lightly. When she woke up, I told her what was going on, and she started to go off. I shushed her and asked her if she still had the teddy bear with the video cam that we used whenever we left the kids overnight at my parent's house. Don't judge me; I was just getting to know them, and I'd be damned if I was sending my kids in blindly. She said that she still had it, so I told her to get Madison's baby bag and pack some pampers, milk, and some of the outfits that we had at the house and to put the teddy bear in the bag. I took Ariel downstairs and handed her over to the female officer and handed the bag over to the male officer that was doing all of the talking.

"Thank you for being cooperative, and like I said, take a trip down to family court with any issues you may have," he said, looking like he wanted me to give him a reason to arrest me.

I didn't even answer the motherfucker. I walked them to the door, and it took everything in me not to go at that bitch, Jasmine, who was standing up against the police car, smirking. I knew this bitch was fucking the officer; her nasty ass was probably fucking both of them. Tasha tried to get pass me to get at the bitch, but I had to remind her that whether those officers were clearly doing Jasmine a favor or not, the fact still remained that they were still real police officers, and she needed to fall back.

I told her not to worry because the teddy bear would give us a location on her. It took me a few minutes, but after the words left my mouth, it dawned on me that we wouldn't be getting any location on her. I'm telling you that this shit had me and Tasha stressed the fuck out because not once at the time that we were discussing the bear did we realize that the teddy bear didn't have a locater. It was just a video cam.

I was so angry that I wanted to punch the fucking wall; the bitch was so close, and I couldn't fucking touch her. I went and sat on the couch with my head in my hands because this was all my fucking fault. The fact that this bitch stayed two fucking steps ahead of us was starting to mess with my head. I looked up, and Tasha handed me a bottle of water with the Tylenol bottle. She sat across from me and popped the two pills that she took from the bottle and drank her bottle of water. She didn't say anything; she just sat there, staring at me with a look of disgust on her face.

"Thank you. I'm sorry for causing all of this bullshit in our relationship, and I promise I'm going to make it right," I said, attempting to get her to talk to me.

"Rellz, this shit is killing me, and I don't know how much more of this I can take before having a breakdown. I'm so tired of you doing me like this. All I've ever done, after my fuck up years ago, was prove to you that this is where I want to be and that you are who I want to be with, but you haven't done the same." She rubbed her temples.

"Tash, that's true, and I know that I fucked up, but please, allow me to make this shit right," I pleaded.

"Rellz, how is this going to work? Yes, it will be another dead bitch, but we can't keep killing bitches every time you decide to fuck someone. Why can't you just respect your wife enough to not fuck other bitches, especially bitches who are connected to my ass," she said, getting emotional.

I wanted to hold her, but I knew that she wasn't going to let me touch her. It was killing me that I just continued to hurt her when she has proven to be nothing but loyal to my ass. I honestly wanted to make it right, but I didn't know how, or where, to even begin.

Chapter Twenty-Three (Jasmine)

That bitch, Tasha, must have thought that I was stupid if she thought I was going to let her play house with my fucking baby. I just wanted to let that bitch know that her fucking cheating man was the father of the child that she thought was just her goddaughter. Tasha had been playing the fool for Rellz way before I came along, and had she not told me all of her fucking business about the dog that he was, I probably would have never pushed up on his weak ass. She's probably going to take his ass back, just like she always did, because she doesn't really want to raise all those kids on her own. Yes, she's able to do it financially, but mentally, she wouldn't be able too. I was just glad that Officer Newman was able to assist me with getting Ariel back from the bitch; my baby served her purpose, and it was time for her to come home. I wasn't giving them any time to try and go to court to keep my baby. The dumb bitch had the nerve to put that damn teddy bear in the bag, like it was going to help their asses. I don't know what the fuck they were thinking, but I laughed my ass off at their expense.

I spent my day watching Lah's every move. It still amazed me that he chose his plain Jane wife over all of this that I had going on over here. That bitch didn't hold a candle to me, and he fucked up when he chose the bitch. All these motherfuckers deserved each other because they were all a bunch of fucking dummies. Looking for someone who was watching them; it was funny as hell to see Rellz run up in Justin's crib when I stopped fucking with that clown because he was another weak faggot that chose his wife over me. All these niggas are about to find out that fucking over Jasmine was the wrong fucking move. Lah's fine ass I might spare, but his bitch might not be so lucky.

I got back to Tony's loft in Brooklyn a little after 6:00 pm, and he was blowing me about leaving him with Ariel all day. He sent me a message in my inbox last month, letting me know that he moved to New York, and he wanted to know if we could somehow mend our friendship. I didn't answer his inbox until I needed a place to stay. I had him believing that we could leave what happened in the past. He could believe that bullshit if he wanted to because I would never forgive him for what he did to me, and as soon as I didn't need his ass anymore, he was going to find out just how much he hurt me in the past. I don't even know why he came to New York, and I blame myself for not having my location set to private on Facebook. If he had seen that I moved anywhere else, his ass wouldn't have even reached out. He's probably playing my ass to see who my man is and if he could fuck that one too, with his skank ass.

He no longer wants to be called Tony with a Y; he's now Toni with an I. When he told me that shit, I looked at him like he was special. Unless you're showing your ID, who the fuck cares how it's spelled? It sounded the damn same. I brushed his ass off about me being gone all day because his ass will have her tomorrow, too. I picked Ariel up and went to the room he was letting me stay in. I knew that he was showing out for his little boy toy that he had over because he knew that he had fallen in love with Ariel's little ass from the first time he laid eyes on my baby. He was probably mad because Ariel kept him from getting his ass stretched wider than it probably already was.

Since I've been here, I wanted to ask him about Que, but I didn't because I didn't want to open up old wounds. It didn't stop me from thinking about him though. Thinking about where we would have been if he wasn't playing for the other team, I often wonder if we would have had children or even been married by now. I got back to the matter at hand and that was undressing my baby and checking her to make sure that everything was everything. I just might use that teddy bear that they put in the bag to watch his fucking ass when he has my baby. I don't think he will do anything to her, but you have some crazy motherfuckers in this fucked up world that we live in. She looked the same as when I left her, so I took her into the bathroom to give her a bath before giving her a bottle for the night. Once I got Ariel down, I went downstairs to get something to eat, and I was happy to see that Toni's company had left.

"Do you want me to make you a sandwich while I'm making me one?" I asked him.

"As long as you're not trying to poison my ass," he said. He must have been reading my mind, but his number wasn't up just yet, so he was good.

"I told you that I'm not harboring any ill feelings about what happened in the past, now stop bringing it up." I pretended to be upset.

"Damn, my bad. When did you become so sensitive?" he questioned, with his hand on his hip.

"I'm not being sensitive. It's just annoying that you allow me to stay here, but you're acting as if you don't trust me," I said, faking being offended.

"Girl, you're good. I was just fucking with you. Remember, no mayonnaise on my sandwich," he said, switching his ass back to the couch.

I tried my best to put a friendly mask on my face, but it was killing me inside to be around his ass. As soon as I no longer need a place to lay low, his ass is going to get what he should have gotten all those years ago. His little fairy ass had the nerve to ask me if he could be Ariel's godmother when we first met up. All I could do was laugh at his big, six-foot busty ass referring to himself as a she. It took everything in me that day not to let him have it.

After the sandwiches were made, I went and joined him in the living room, and I'm not going to lie, it almost felt like old times when we were friends. We laughed and talked about the old neighborhood, including when I had to take a bat to some of the neighborhood boys who were fucking with him about being gay. That's why it was so hard to believe that he would do me like that; I always had his back - no matter what. Even when my mom tried to forbid me from hanging with him, because of all the trouble that came with being his friend, did I listen and stop being his friend? Hell no.

It was time for me to excuse myself and take my ass to bed so I could get ready for my next move on making those fuck boys pay for what they did to me. I was hoping Chink's aunt broke her fucking neck when she fell down those fucking stairs, but she didn't, so I decided to just let her be and ride with her to the hospital to let Chink's ass know that this was only the beginning.

"So, you're not going to even ask about him?" he asked me, interrupting my thoughts.

"Ask about him?" I asked, pretending like I didn't know who he was talking about.

"Girl, your ass knows who I'm talking about. So, you don't want to know what happened to Que?" he asked.

"To be honest with you, I wasn't really thinking about his ass," I lied, with a straight face.

"Yeah, okay. You must have forgotten that I know you better than you know yourself," he replied.

"I doubt that because, if you knew me better than I knew myself, you wouldn't have slept with my man to begin with," I said, getting pissed off.

"I'm going to let you have that one because I understand that bringing him up has you feeling some kind of way. So, anyway," he replied, with a roll of the eyes.

I was a few seconds from snatching that damn head scarf off of his damn head, sitting there looking like Goldmouth from the movie *Life*.

"Well, if you don't want to know what happened to Que, then take your ass to bed, but I promise you, you want to hear this tea," he smiled.

"Okay, me hearing about Que is going to benefit me how?" I asked him.

166

"I'm not saying that it's going to benefit you, but like I said, I know that you want to know what happened to his ass."

"Okay, Toni. Enlighten me since you're not going to let me go to bed without telling me."

"Girl, after you left his ass and the neighborhood started talking, he wanted to prove to everyone that he wasn't gay, so he started acting all thuggish and shit, getting hooked up with the wrong people. He was slinging those thangs and ended up getting locked up, serving fifteen years. After he got locked up, girl, I cut that ass off and took his bank, that he had stashed with me, and that's why I'm in New York," he said, in all one breath. He didn't know that he had fucked up with that information that he felt he could trust me with.

"Toni, your ass ain't shit. You know his ass needed his stash to keep money on his books." We both laughed.

"That's exactly why he told me where the stash was to begin with, but my ass ain't no damn fool; I got ghost on his ass. If he thought that I was going to do a fifteen year bid with his ass, he must have been smoking that shit that he was slinging." He laughed while my mind went into overdrive, wondering where he could be hiding the money at in his crib.

"Girl, I'm taking my ass to bed. I'm not fucking with you, and don't come looking for my bag because I sleep with my shit," I said, laughing.

"Whatever, trick," he said, throwing the pillow off the couch at me.

Once I made it to the room, all I could think about was where he was hiding that money because he was definitely coming up off of that. I moved Ariel closer to the middle of the bed. It looked like she had moved because I could have sworn that I left her in the middle, and she was now lying closer to the edge of the bed. I placed a pillow on both sides of her while I went to take a shower before calling it a night. I had all my shit in storage, but if this faggot was sitting on some real change, I would be getting my shit sooner than I thought. I hated to give up my place, but I knew that Rellz and Lah would be coming for me after all the shit that I started. That's why I made sure to stay two steps ahead of their asses.

That shower was everything, and my body was relaxed and ready to hit that pillow as soon as I got my ass into bed. Before calling it a night, I had to run back downstairs to get Ariel's pacifier because, without a doubt, she would be whining for it early in the damn morning. I have been trying to get her ass on a better schedule, but it wasn't working.

Sometimes I wished that her father was a man that belonged to me because I yearned for that someone to help share in her early morning feedings and pamper changes.

Toni's ass fell asleep on the couch, watching the television, like he had been doing every night since I've been here, which tells me that the money had to be hidden somewhere in his living room. That fucking living room was so big that it could be hidden behind anything. I know that his ass didn't fully trust me like he pretended to, but it's all good. He will soon enough. I took my ass upstairs, got in bed with my daughter, and dreamed about my come up.

Chapter Twenty-Four (Polo)

I just pulled up to the grocery store. Tonight, I was making dinner for Liem to show him how much I appreciated him. After watching what Chink and Tasha had been going through, it only made me appreciate him more. The fact that he made his mistake and learned from it showed me how much he had matured, and it only made me love him more. I took Paris from the car seat and carried her to the supermarket, strapping her into the shopping cart. The supermarket wasn't too crowded, so I should be in and out in no time. I just needed the ingredients for my lasagna, and I also needed to get garlic bread.

I rolled my cart to the aisle that carried the pasta, and just as I was about to reach for what I needed, my phone rang. It was my mother, so I used my shoulder to hold the phone in place, while I turned to pull two boxes of pasta down. I then walked a little toward the end of the aisle to grab a few jars of sauce. When I turned to walk back to the cart, it was gone. I dropped the jars that I was holding in my hands, along with the pasta and my phone. I started to panic as I ran frantically, going from aisle to aisle, looking for my cart that had my daughter inside.

By this time, everyone knew that my daughter was missing because I was screaming at the top of my lungs. I couldn't breathe, but it didn't stop me from running around the store like a chicken with my head cut off. I heard the announcement over the intercom, letting everyone know that a child was missing. They also placed the store on lockdown. By this time, I started to hyperventilate and really couldn't breathe. I had to sit on the store floor as a few of the patrons tried to comfort me.

"Ma'am, is this your child?" I heard someone say.

I looked up to see one of the customers holding a smiling Paris in her arms. I jumped up quickly and took my baby out of her arms, kissing her all over her face. I now cried happy tears as I thanked everyone for helping me look for my daughter. The manager tried to convince me that I might have forgotten that I left her in the aisle that she was found in, but I knew that I left my cart and baby in the same aisle that I was in. I knew for a fact that I didn't walk to another aisle; she was in the same aisle, and he wasn't going to convince me otherwise. Somebody moved her.

One of the customers handed me my phone, and after using my shirt to wipe off the spaghetti sauce that covered it, I called Liem. I let him know what happened as I walked to the car. The manager wanted me to stay and look at the video after I told him that I was positive that I didn't leave my baby alone in another aisle, but I declined. I just wanted to get my baby home. I was an emotional wreck, and Liem could hardly understand what I was saying. I walked over to my car, and there was a note attached to my back door window. After reading the note that basically said that, "Next time you won't be so lucky," I knew that it was Jasmine, and I was just about sick of this bitch.

I calmed myself down enough to call Liem back, and he was pissed. He told me to go home and to make sure that I locked all the doors. I called Chink to let her know what happened, and she told me that she was leaving the shop. She was so upset that she was crying, and I found myself consoling her. I loved my sis, but she was such a crybaby. I looked back at my baby in the rearview mirror, and I thanked God that the crazy bitch didn't walk out of the supermarket with her. When I pulled up in my driveway, I looked around, making sure that it was safe before taking Paris out of the car and going inside to wait on Liem and Chink to get here.

Liem walked in the door about twenty minutes after I did, and I had never seen him this angry before. He was so mad that he was stuttering. His questions to me were kind of aggressive, and I let it slide because I knew that he was upset, but when it started to feel like he was blaming me, I had to shut him down for a second and bring him back to the matter at hand. I had to remind him that Paris was okay and that it wasn't my fault that this crazy bitch was running around fucking with our family. He dialed Lah's number and left out of the room but not before taking Paris with him like I was going to lose her again. Chink finally got here, and she was able to calm him down, telling him that pointing the finger wasn't going to do anything but cause us to go at each other. She said that we all just needed to thank God that Paris was safe because the situation could have been worse.

"I'm sorry, babe," he said, taking me in his arms.

"It's okay. I shouldn't have left her, even if it was just for a second," I cried, tears falling.

"No, don't go blaming yourself, and like I said, I'm sorry. I shouldn't have blamed you. This is all Jasmine's fault, and she needs to be dealt with." He was getting angry all over again as he wiped my tears.

"This shit is really getting out of control; I think it's time we go to the police," Chink said, and as much as I didn't want to, I agreed with her.

"Nah, we just have to be smarter about this shit. The bitch has to have been following us to know our every fucking move. We are not about to involve the police; we're going to handle this," Liem responded.

I wasn't convinced, but I had no choice but to take his word for it. I agreed with him that she had to be watching us to know our every move because how else would she have known that I was at the supermarket? Chink stayed, waiting on Lah to arrive because he told her that he didn't want her to drive home without him. He wasn't able to leave work earlier when Liem left, so he was just getting off of work and was on his way to pick her up to follow her home. I wasn't able to make what I wanted to for dinner, so Chink and I went into the kitchen to whip up something so that we could at least have a meal before they left. None of us were really in the mood to eat, but it did take the edge off of what we were all feeling.

Liem refused to let Paris out of his sight, and he refused to put her down. I couldn't blame him though because that few minutes of not knowing where my baby was had me terrified. I didn't even know how to tell my mother what had happened today because she would freak out for sure; this shit was so stressful.

Once Lah and Chink left, I went upstairs to take a shower to try and relive some of the pressure that I was feeling. Usually Tylenol works, but tonight, it did nothing for the headache that was invading me right now. I can honestly say that I have never hated anyone the way I hated Jasmine's ass right now. I did nothing to her that she didn't deserve, so for her to come after my child really had me thinking about killing her ass. I was starting to think that something else was going on with her ass because I'm finding it really hard to believe that she is going this hard over some dick that never belonged to her ass. I don't know how Tasha had been friends with her ass all this time and couldn't tell that she was off in the fucking head. Crazy doesn't just happen overnight; she had to have been always fucking crazy. I came out of the shower, and Liem and Paris were in the bed. I guess he wasn't going to let her sleep in her room tonight, and I was with him on that.

The next morning, Liem didn't want to go to work and leave us at home alone, so I told him that he could take me to my mother's house, and I would stay there until he picked me up after work. I decided not to say anything to my mother about what had happened because I didn't need her worrying and telling me that I needed to stay with her. It was like 8:00 am when I got to her house, so I just used my key because she knew that I was coming. She still worked at night, so I told her that it was okay to go to bed and that I would let myself in. Liem pulled off once Paris and I were inside safely. They need to deal with Jasmine soon because me leaving work to be a stay at home mom didn't include me running from my house every day or needing a babysitter every time I needed to leave the house.

"Hey, Mom. I thought you would be sleeping?" I said to her as she came down the stairs.

"No, I was waiting on you to get here. Are you and Liem having problems?" she asked, giving me a hug.

"No, Mom. We're not having problems. It just gets lonely being home all day with just Paris and me, so I wanted to come and sit with you today," I said, hating to lie to my mom.

"Okay, well make yourself at home while I make us some breakfast."

"Mom, you don't have to make me breakfast," I insisted.

"Cool. I won't make you breakfast, but I'm still going to make me something to eat," she laughed.

"Well, make me some too if you're going to cook anyway," I said, walking out of the kitchen.

I enjoyed spending the day with my mom. We spent all day watching all the talk shows, and when those ended, we watched the court shows. Liem called like a million times to check up on us; I had to tell him that I was going to kick his butt if he called me one more time. I couldn't even be mad at him because Chink called just as much as he did, and I didn't threaten her to stop calling. Liem got to my mom's house at exactly 6:30pm. I kissed my mom bye and told her that I would call her when we got to the house. When we got home,

I gave the baby to Liem so that I could wash my hands and start dinner.

My phone alerted me that I had a text message, and it was from an unknown number again. I have been getting these text messages almost every day, and they started way before Jasmine's ass started with her bullshit, so I wasn't sure who the text messages were from. I didn't say anything to anyone because I didn't think anything of it, but they were getting crazier by the day. The one that I just received was asking me if I enjoyed my time with my mother today, and then it went on to say that they always liked my mother. It was really freaking me out. Last month, I had to deactivate my Instagram page because someone named Jigga was stalking the hell out of my page and leaving inappropriate comments. Once I deactivated the page, that's when the text messages started. I wanted to change my number, but if I did that, Liem was going to want to know why I changed my number, and I didn't want to alarm him with the reason why. I know that I shouldn't keep secrets from him, and I'm going to tell him eventually, but I want to speak to Chink about it first.

It's been a few weeks without incident, so Liem has let up a little, and my princess and me were on our way to meet with Chink for lunch without security detail. I pulled out of the driveway, and as soon as I got about a block away from home, the car shut off. I pressed down on the gas. Nothing. I didn't know what the hell was going on, but I couldn't, for the life of me, get the car to start. I looked into my rearview mirror, and a car was stopping behind me. I didn't need any assistance, so I put my hand out of the window, telling the driver to go around and keep moving. I guess the driver didn't understand what I was trying to say, and I watch as he stepped out of the car. I could tell it was a man because he was wearing jeans and a sweatshirt, with a fitted pulled down, covering his face. By the time I realized who the driver was, it was too late for me to lock all of the doors as he pulled the driver's side door open.

"Jared, what the hell are you doing here?" I asked him.

"Get out of the car, and you better not scream," he demanded as I looked at him like he was fucking stupid.

"Jared, I'm not about to get out of the car. What do you want?" I asked him.

"Patricia, you have three seconds to get out of the fucking car before I yank you out by your hair," he said, aggressively.

I looked around to see if anyone would come to my rescue if I screamed, but I didn't see anyone. I could have tried to fight him off, but I didn't want to jeopardize my daughter's life or my own by putting up a fight. I removed my seat belt and stepped out of the car. I walked towards the back of the car, attempting to pull the door open to get Paris out, but he grabbed me by my arm, stopping me.

"Leave the baby, and walk to my car. I swear if you put up a fight, she's dead," he said.

"Jared, are you fucking crazy? I'm not about to leave my baby in the car alone." My tears began to fall at the thought of leaving her.

"Move now!" he shouted, now showing me the gun that he had in his hand that I didn't notice before.

My mind was telling me to move, but my legs wouldn't allow me to as I begged him to let me take Paris with me. He forced me to the car by pushing me with the gun in my back. If he hadn't threatened my baby's life, I would have died trying to fight him, but like I said, I couldn't risk it, so he no longer had to push, and I walked to the car. Once in the passenger seat, I prayed that someone would come along and notice her in the car before it was too late. I tried to plead with him one last time, but he hit me in the head with the gun, causing my neck to jerk back, and then, darkness.

Chapter Twenty-Five (Chink)

Polo was late for our lunch date, and had it only been a few minutes, I wouldn't have worried, but she was almost an hour late. I called her phone numerous times, and I didn't want to alarm Liem by calling him, but I had to let him know what was going on. Before calling Liem, I decided to call Lah first because he always said that I tend to blow things out of proportion.

"Hey, babe," he said, answering the call.

"Babe, Polo and I had a lunch date today, but she never showed. She's not answering her phone, so I'm starting to worry. I didn't know if I should let Liem know because it might be nothing," I said.

"Well, any other time, I would say not to worry, but with all that's been going on, I say that we should worry. I'm going to go and get Liem, and we will go to the house just to make sure that she didn't fall asleep. I will call you as soon as we get to the house," he said.

"No way will I be able to sit here at work, not knowing if she is okay or not. I'm going to leave and meet you at their house," I informed him, grabbing my bag and ending the call before he told me to stay put.

I was about fifteen minutes away from their place when my phone rang. It was Lah calling, so I took a deep breath before answering the call.

"Hey, babe. Was she at the house?" I asked, nervously.

"No, babe. We found her car a block away from the house, with Paris still strapped in her car seat; she's okay. When we located the car, she was sleeping. We don't know how long she was left in the car, but her body temperature was still warm, so it wasn't too long. Liem is on the phone with 911 as we speak," he said.

"I'm not too far away. I'll be there in like fifteen minutes." I cried.

"Babe, try to calm down and make it here safely. We're going to find her," he said as I ended the call.

When I got to the house, there were two police cars out front. Once inside, I saw Liem talking to the officers, and Lah holding Paris. I went and took the baby from him and held on to her for dear life as the tears fell from my eyes. I called Polo's mom and Tasha, and they both said that they were on their way. Liem told the police about everything that had been happening with all that Jasmine had been doing, but we really didn't have any concrete evidence because Tasha got rid of the letter in a fit of rage, and my aunt's description wasn't enough. So basically they said that there would be a search for her, and they are going to tow the car to look for any evidence, which meant they weren't going to do shit.

Now, we all sat around, brainstorming and trying to figure out where to start looking; we really had no clue where to start. Liem went and unlocked the door for Tasha and Rellz. I was silently pissed off at Lah and Rellz because had they kept their fucking dicks in their pants, this shit wouldn't be happening. However, I kept my feelings to myself because right now that wouldn't help bring Polo home. Rellz shared with us that he had gone through something similar with Tasha, and he found her by tracking her cell phone.

Liem went to see if Polo's cell phone was in her bag, and it wasn't. He checked the baby's bag, and it wasn't in there either, so he gave Rellz her cell phone number. Rellz was going to call his connect to see if we could get a location on her. I started to feel hopeful, but I was still doubtful at the same time. I tried to comfort Polo's mom because she kept crying and repeating that she knew that something was going on when Polo stayed with her every day until Liem picked her up. Then, she started blaming herself for not prying, and I decided not to tell her exactly why Jasmine was doing all of the things that she was doing.

We just told her that Tasha and Jasmine had a falling out because she chose to be friends with Polo and me and not her anymore. I took Paris upstairs to get her washed and put her down; LJ was in one of the bedrooms, already sleeping. It was getting late, and Rellz said that he probably wouldn't hear anything from the person who was getting the location until some time tomorrow. Polo's mom stayed at the house with Paris and Liem, while the rest of us all headed out. I didn't want to leave, but there was nothing else that I could do by sitting there, so I let Lah talk me into going home.

I didn't get any sleep. I was up all night thinking about whether Polo was okay or not. Just the thought of her laying somewhere hurt, or even dead, was really stressing me the hell out. I found myself calling all of the hospitals that I could think of to see if she was at any of them, but no one had her listed or even a Jane Doe that fit her description. The next morning, I was sitting in the living room with LJ, watching *Penguins of Madagascar* on DVD, when Lah came downstairs, dressed in all black.

"What's going on?" I asked him, noticing he was strapped.

"Rellz called. We have a location," he said, causing me to jump up and begin putting on my sneakers.

"Whoa, babe. What are you doing?" he asked, looking at me like I was crazy.

"I'm going with you," I responded, tying my laces.

"Chink, you're not going. Rellz is on his way with Liem to get me, and Tasha and the kids are going to stay here with you and LJ until we bring Polo home," he said.

I was disappointed that I wasn't able to go, but once I thought about it, if Tasha and I went with them, who was going to watch the kids? I didn't want to stay back and play the waiting game, but I trusted my man to bring my friend home. I was thanking God that her phone hadn't died because had it died, the dude wouldn't have been able to get a location. Once Tasha and the kids got inside, we locked the doors, and the guys were on their way to bring Polo home. I prayed that they all made it back safely.

Chapter Twenty-Six (Polo)

I woke up with a banging headache. I tried to adjust my eyes to the light that was coming from the window. I looked around and noticed that I was at Jared's place. I looked around, but he was nowhere in sight, so I got up to run to the door. I turned the knob a few times to no avail and noticed that I needed a key to get out of the house.

"You're trying to leave me again?" I heard his voice behind me.

"Jared, why the fuck do you have me here?" I asked him.

I started to feel lightheaded as I leaned up against the door; he came over and helped me back to the couch. He never answered my question; he just kept caressing my face and staring at me, freaking me out.

"Jared, I need to leave here and get back to my family. I need to know if my daughter is okay," I pleaded.

"Fuck that. You were supposed to have my baby, not that nigga's baby. He fucked around on you and got the next bitch pregnant, or did you forget about that?" he yelled, with spittle flying in my face.

"Jared, we were just friends. Nothing more, nothing less," I said.

"So, you let all of your friends perform oral sex on you?" he shouted in my face.

I was really starting to worry now because I don't know what the fuck he had fixated in his mind, but that never happened. Yes, I had come to his house on a couple occasions, and I even kissed him a few times, but him going down on me never happened.

"Jared, I don't know what you're talking about. That never happened. I slipped up and kissed you, but I quickly pushed you away when I realized what I was doing. I told you that I was in love with Liem then, and I'm still in love with him now," I said.

"So, you're trying to say that you were playing with my fucking emotions?" he yelled as he slapped me in my face. "See what you made me do? I don't want to hurt you," he said, caressing my face again.

I had never seen this side of him, and he was starting to scare me with this good guy/bad guy routine he had going on. He was always so nice to me, and he never showed me that he possessed a bad side. Even when he was stressed out at work, he never got angry or anything. I heard my phone vibrating, and he heard it too.

"What the fuck is that? You have a cell phone?" he asked. He started checking me until he found the phone. "Did you call someone? Didn't I tell you to leave all of your belongings in the car?" he said, slapping me again, this time knocking me off the couch.

I grabbed my face, and I swear I saw red. I was about to hit his ass back, but he was now on his knees, with his gun pointed in my face. He told me that the next time that I didn't do as he told me, he was going to make sure that I ended up in a body bag.

"I love you, and you keep making me hurt you. Why do you keep making me hurt you?" he asked, shaking the gun in my face.

He stood up, took my phone, and stepped on it continuously until it shattered all over the floor.

"Jared, I just want to go home. My family is probably worried about me. Please, just let me go," I pleaded with him.

"I'm supposed to be your family. That's supposed to be my baby that you were carrying."

"Jared, how many times do I have to tell you that I love Liem, and in case you forgot, you loved Dymond?" I said, and it sent him in a frenzy.

I watched as he started destroying his place. He picked up the lamp and threw it into the television, chanting over and over again that Dymond left him just like I left him. This nigga had to be some kind of crazy. Dymond was killed; she didn't leave him voluntarily, and my ass was never with him. We were only friends, and I didn't know how many times I needed to stress that to him, so I decided to try a different approach.

"Jared, we were friends. You knew my situation, but you failed to share your situation with me. We could have continued to be friends, but that ended when you lied to me," I said to him, but I didn't get a reaction. He just paced the floor, with the gun still in his hand, like he was contemplating his next move.

"Jared, you have too much to lose by doing this. Just let me go, and I promise you that I won't tell anyone what happened today," I continued.

He looked like he was thinking about what I had just said, and I was hopeful that he was going to let me go, until he walked back over to me, caressing my thigh. I was praying that this nigga wasn't going to try and rape my ass. My face was still stinging from the slaps that he delivered to my face, and I could feel the dry blood on the top of my head from where he hit me with the gun. I didn't need him violating my body to add to all that he had done to me already.

I tried my best to plead to him with my eyes to not do this. If he had ever felt anything for me, he wouldn't do this to me. He avoided eye contact as his hand massaged my breast through my shirt. I pushed his hand, just to be slapped again, and this time, I kicked him as hard as I could, knocking him off the couch. I jumped up, trying to make it upstairs to one of the rooms, hoping that one of them had a lock on it. I made it up about four steps before he was pulling me back down by my hair. He was now straddling me and punching me all over my body. He caused the gash on my head to open back up as the blood now dripped down the side of my face. I was trying to fight him as best I could, but I was feeling lightheaded, and my punches had no effect on him, only causing him to hit me harder.

I stopped fighting, and that's when he let up with the abuse. I laid in the fetal position as he started pacing the floor again. I was starting to believe that I wasn't going to get out of this alive, but that was before I heard glass shattering. It sounded like it was coming from the kitchen area, and I watched as Jared picked up the gun from the sofa and headed in the direction that the noise came from.

Chapter Twenty-Seven (Liem)

My adrenaline was working overtime once we pulled up to the address where my wife was supposed to be being held. The plan was to wait it out for a few minutes, but I jumped out of the car with Rellz and Lah having no choice but to follow. I went straight to the back of the house, and without thinking about neighbors or what was waiting for me behind the door, I picked up the chair, that was sitting on the back porch, and threw it through the window. I climbed through the window, cutting my leg in the process but not caring. Once inside, I unlocked the back door. I pulled out my gun and began walking through the kitchen area.

We heard movement, so Rellz stood to the side of the refrigerator, and I whispered for Lah to stay by the back door. When he walked in the kitchen, I couldn't believe who I was seeing; it was motherfucking Jared who snatched my fucking wife. The rage took on a mind of its own as I rushed him, causing him to drop the gun that he had in his hand. I beat him to a pulp with my gun repeatedly, until he was no longer moving. I was covered in blood, heaving up and down like a madman. I almost forgot about my wife for a second because I was already thinking about the two bullets that I was about to put in that faggot's head.

"Liem, go and look for your wife. We've got it from here," Lah said to me, snapping me out of my rage.

I walked into the living room, and my wife was lying on the floor in pain. I ran over to her, and when I saw her face, tears of anger ran from my eyes. I picked her up, as gently as I could without hurting her, and carried her through the kitchen. When she saw Jared on the floor, she buried her face into my neck. I wanted to put her down and beat his ass some more, but I needed to get her out of the house.

"Yo, I know this motherfucker. He was my cousin, Dymond's, boyfriend before she was killed," Rellz said to me as he walked over to where Jared was lying unconscious on the floor. "What the fuck made him snatch your brother's wife?" he asked again. He sounded confused, but it was pissing me off because we didn't have time for this shit.

"It's a long story that we don't have time to explain. Let's body this faggot and get the fuck out of here," Lah said to him when he saw the look on my face.

I stepped over Jared's body and made my way out of the back door. I turned back to make sure that they were good and witnessed Lah putting his gun to Jared's head and pulling the trigger. Rellz made a call once we were back in the car, and he told whoever he was talking to to make sure it was clean. I held my wife tight as she whimpered from the pain that she was in. I told Lah to take us to the hospital, but she declined, saying that she just wanted to go home. Rellz called Tasha to let her and Chink know that we had her and that we were taking her home.

When we got to the house, Polo's mom met us at the door, and when she saw her daughter, she cried. I carried her upstairs to the bedroom with her mother following. Polo kept asking for Paris, but her mother told her to get cleaned up first. Her motherly instincts kicked in as she started to tend to Polo's wounds. I went into the bathroom and ran her a bath. Her mother told me that she would assist her in the bathroom and asked me to lie out something for her to put on once she was out of the tub. I wanted to be the one in there with her, but I let her mother do what she do. I laid out some panties and a nightgown before going back downstairs with Rellz and Lah to thank them. Tasha and Chink were walking in the door when I got downstairs, with all the kids in tow.

"Where is she?" Chink cried.

"She's upstairs with her mom; she's in the tub and will be out in a few," I said.

"So was it that bitch Jasmine who had her? I hope you killed the bitch," she asked, upset and forgetting that the kids were in the room with us.

"It wasn't Jasmine. It was Jared who had her," I said, and she gasped.

I put the television on the Cartoon Network so that the kids would be occupied while the grown-ups went into the kitchen to talk. Tasha told the twins to keep an eye out on the younger children as we exited the living room.

"Okay, so why the fuck did Jared, who was the boyfriend of my deceased cousin, kidnap your wife?" Rellz asked.

"I always knew that motherfucker was crazy, and it wouldn't surprise me if he had something to do with Dymond being killed," Tasha said, rolling her eyes.

"Jared and Polo worked at the same job. We were having some problems, and Polo confided in him, and they became friends. She said that nothing happened between them, and they were just friends, but when she found out he was dating Dymond, they fell out because he lied to her. Does it makes sense for him to be upset if the two of them weren't messing around? No, it doesn't, but that's neither here or there. I'm just happy that we got her back home safe where she belongs. I don't know why he snatched her; I guess I have to wait until she's ready to tell me," I explained, kind of getting caught in my feelings.

"Damn, that's some crazy shit. I wish it was Jasmine who snatched her because the bitch would be dead, and this shit would be over. Now we're back to square one concerning that bitch," Rellz said.

Chink excused herself to go upstairs. I'm surprised she refrained from going up as long as she did. Tasha went back into the living room to check on the kids, so I took this time to thank Rellz and my brother for helping me bring my wife home. I knew that my mind shouldn't have been on the reason why he would snatch my wife, but it was. My insecurities started to kick in, just like they did back then, and had me wondering if she really did sleep with him. I tried to clear my head because now wasn't the time to be doubting my wife, but it was hard because the shit just didn't add up.

I had so many questions, but I knew that I had to be sensitive with my approach, and if she wasn't ready to tell me what happened, I needed to respect her decision and wait until she was ready. I pulled out a bottle of Hennessey and shared a drink with Rellz and Lah, trying to calm my nerves. The thought of almost losing her was weighing heavily on my mind; she and Paris were my world, and without them in it, who knows where I'd be? I forgot that I needed to call my mom and sister to let them know that we found her safely.

I went upstairs to check on my wife, and she was sleeping. Chink was lying on one side of her with Polo's mom lying on the other side of her. I signaled for them both to follow me out of the room.

"Hey, I think we should let her get some rest, and everyone meet back up here tomorrow," I suggested once they came out of the room.

"That's cool because she's probably down for the night, so I'm going to go and be back tomorrow. Love you, bro," Chink said, giving me a hug.

"I'm going to take Paris with me tonight, so you can solely be there for my daughter, if that's okay with you?" Polo's mom asked.

"No problem. Let me get her bag packed," I said, thankful that I could just lay in bed with my wife and hold her.

After everyone left, I made sure that all the doors and windows were secured before going upstairs to be with my wife. She was whimpering in her sleep, so I pulled off my clothes, minus my boxers, and pulled her into my arms, holding her close until I dozed off

Chapter Twenty-Eight (Tasha)

I decided to let Rellz spend the night because, I'm not going to lie, I was a little shaken up and wanted him home with me and the children. We put the kids down together, not really saying much to each other. I silently watched him do his fatherly duties, and I was getting turned on. I love my husband and would love for things to go back to the way they were when we got back together after our first real break-up. We were able to put all the obstacles behind us, but this time, I'm not sure. My heart is telling me to give him another chance, but my head is telling me to leave it alone. After all of the kids were in bed, I grabbed what I needed to go and take a shower to relieve some of the stress that I was feeling at the moment. I felt like I was being pulling in two different directions. I stepped in the shower once the temperature was to my liking, and I let the water caress my body.

I heard the shower door being opened, and I was now staring at a naked Rellz. My heartbeat started beating rapidly as my mouth watered at this fine specimen of a man. I tried to tell myself to be strong and tell him to get out of the shower, but instead, I became the aggressor. I pulled him to me and stuck my tongue in his mouth. Visions of him fucking Jasmine tried to enter my mental, but I ignored them as he lifted me up and sat me on his dick. I wrapped my arms around his neck and fucked him in a bench-pressing motion. I was trying to prove to him that I was that bitch as I hopped off the dick and deep throated his ass as the water hit my back. He grabbed me by my hair and forced himself deeper, and I was taking it like a champ.

Just as I was getting into it, he pulled me up and positioned me away from the water. He placed my hands on the wall as he pulled my hips into him, entering me with deep, long strokes. I was screaming his name as I felt myself about to cum. I was seconds away from cumming, and he stopped fucking me. I wanted to scream, but it was short lived as he stuck his tongue in my ass. I backed my ass up on his tongue as he fingered my pussy, and the nut that was begging to be released was released with me screaming out in pleasure. He entered me again, this time with no mercy as he banged the pussy out. The shit hurt so good as he came hard, holding on to my hips. He continued to pump inside of me until he was empty. We washed each other and exited the bathroom; we both passed out on the bed, naked as the day we were born.

I woke up the next morning, not knowing how to feel about giving Rellz the ass last night. I felt that I gave in to him once again, without any real consequences. He was still sleeping, snoring loudly, as I just lay in bed, watching him. I heard the kids up and about, so I decided to get out of bed and get their breakfast started. I was sitting on the couch with the kids, who were all fed and now watching television quietly. Rellz came downstairs and joined me on the loveseat, and just like I knew it would be, the atmosphere felt awkward and uncomfortable at the same time.

"No breakfast for the king?" he asked.

"You were sleeping, and I didn't want to wake you, so I put your plate in the microwave," I said nervously. I felt like I was talking to a stranger that I just had a one-night stand with.

"Can I ask you a question?" I asked him.

"You just did," he joked. "I'm just kidding. What's up?" he continued.

"I don't want to say that last night was a mistake because I wanted it, and I enjoyed it. But I need to know where do we go from here?" I asked him.

He got up, grabbed my hand, and pulled me with him to the den. I guess he didn't want to have this conversation in front of the kids. I felt safe having the conversation in front of the kids because I knew that I wouldn't get emotional in front of them. I sat down on the sofa, and he sat with me, taking my hands into his.

"Tash, I don't know where we go from here because I know that you're going to find it hard to believe me when I say that it will never happen again," he started, but I interrupted him.

"Rellz, I'm not focused on if it will happen again right now. I'm more interested in why it keeps happening? What is it that I do to push you in the arms of another woman? This is the second time you've slept with someone that I considered a friend. Not that it would make me feel any different if it was a stranger, but if you're going to cheat, why don't you have enough respect for me not to cheat with someone who is not connected to me?" I asked him.

"Tash, I know the 'it just happened' line is played out, but it's the truth. Jasmine came on to me, one thing led to another, and we slept together. I realized that I fucked up after that first time, and I told her that it couldn't happen again. She threatened me, telling me that she would tell you if I cut her off," he said.

"So, instead of getting some balls and telling me yourself, you continued to sleep with her unprotected, had a baby, and continued to sleep with her even after you found out that she was sleeping with Lah. Even after he got caught, you continued to sleep with her. Can you explain that?" I asked him because I really didn't understand.

He didn't answer right away; he just sat there like he was thinking of how to answer the question. It was pissing me off because, if he wasn't going to try to tell me another bullshit lie, answering the question should have been easy to answer instead of pausing. I wanted to have faith that he could change, but honestly, I don't think he's ever going to change.

"Tash, I don't want to lie to you," he said.

"Rellz, then don't. No matter what you think will happen, I want you to tell me the truth," I said, looking him in his eyes.

"Okay, I'm going to keep it real with you. The first time that I slept with Jasmine, she did things to my body that had me craving her touch. It was supposed to be me just hitting and quitting it, but I got hooked and even started having feelings for her. When she got pregnant with Ariel, I wanted us to be a family. It sounds fucked up, but that's how she had a nigga feeling. I was going to leave you for her, but she didn't want to be with me like that. I believe she just got off on fucking with a married man. I was feeling some kind of way when she rejected me, so I asked her to get rid of the baby, and she declined. Like I said, she did something to me, and I just couldn't leave her alone, so I continued to sleep with her. Once she started messing with Lah, it pissed me off but not enough for me to stop messing with her. Jasmine isn't doing all of this because of me. She's fucking with us because Lah stopped fucking with her, and you stopped being her friend. None of what she's doing has to do with her wanting to be with me," he explained, putting his head into his hands.

I wanted the truth, but I never expected him to say that he was going to leave me for that bitch. So he was really feeling her like that, but he continued to tell me that he loved me, and he was happy being with the kids and me. I knew that he was waiting for me to respond, but I didn't know how to respond because I was angry, hurt, and felt sick to my stomach that he cared for someone more than he cared for me and the kids. Tears stung at my eyes at the thought that the man that I loved with my all was going to leave me if my ex-best friend wanted his ass. The tears fell, and he wiped them from my face, asking me not to cry. I didn't want to cry because he didn't deserve my tears, but the pain I was feeling really hurt me - physically and emotionally.

"Tash, please stop crying; I'm sorry. You asked for the truth, and I gave it to you," he said.

"Rellz, never in a million years would I have believed that you would leave me and our kids for another woman because you fell in love with the way she fucked you. Or, was that a lie too, and you fell in love with her?" I asked him.

"Tash, I didn't love her. I love you, and I want to be with you. If you just give me another chance, I swear I will do whatever it takes to prove to you that home is where I want to be," he insisted.

Sometimes I wished that you could just turn love off. Rellz didn't deserve me, but it didn't stop me from continuing to love him with all of his faults. I have taken unconditional love too far by allowing him to cheat on me, over and over again, and taking him back. I kept telling myself that if I left for good and broke up our family, the kids would suffer. I know my mom is looking down on me, very disappointed right now. She told me so many times that love didn't hurt, but here I was, once again, hurting at the hands of a man who said he loved me but continued to hurt me.

I tried my best to stop the tears from falling, but they wouldn't stop because they had a mind of their own. Rellz pulled me into his arms, holding me tight, and whispering in my ear that he would never hurt me again and to please just give him one more chance. I have always been a fool for love when it came to this man, and I swear I just wanted the pain to stop. My heart hurt, and even though I knew that Rellz would never change, I convinced myself that I needed him.

"I love you, Tash," he whispered in my ear.

"I love you too, Rellz," I said, burying my face into his chest.

We got up and went back into the living room with the kids and watched television with them. Madison climbed in between us and sat on her daddy's lap with RJ following her and sitting on my lap. I know that a person on the outside looking in wouldn't understand, but I loved my family, and if staying with my cheating husband and having their father in the home with us meant keeping a smile on my kids' faces, then that was what I was going to do. He wrapped his free arm around me and pulled me to him, and I laid my head on his shoulder, closing my eyes and silently crying on the inside.

Chapter Twenty-Nine (Jasmine)

It took me two months to find Toni's stash, and when I did, I couldn't believe how much bank he was sitting on. I used that damn teddy bear every day since the day he told me that he took Que's money, and every day that I watched the footage, I was disappointed. That was until he got sprung on his new boy toy. He was taking him to the Bahamas and needed money to trick on his ass for the trip. I sat on my bed, looking at the footage. I watched as he moved the statue that sat in the corner of the living room. He lifted the floorboard and pulled out a black duffel bag, opening it up and pulling out a few stacks. He then placed the bag back and put the board and statue back in place. I would have never found that money if I was just searching the living room because that hiding spot was genius. Anyone visiting or living there would have never known that the floorboard lifted. Lucky for his ass, I didn't have to kill him like I originally planned to; I swear I was going to poison his ass. I still had to wait him out because he wasn't leaving for the Bahamas until the following day. I played nice and tried not to act suspicious as he gave me all of his rules for his place before he left to leave for the airport.

Once he left for the airport, I waited a few hours before hitting his hiding place. My eyes lit up when I noticed that it wasn't just one but two black duffel bags. I took the bags, my baby, and we bounced; I took a cab to a hotel where Ariel and I stayed that first night. I counted the money, and when I counted one hundred grand, my ass was no longer interested in any of my earlier plans to find a place and get my stuff out of storage. I had enough money to start over and say fuck everyone that had fucked me over because if my ass was in jail or dead, I wouldn't get to spend my newfound wealth.

I did something that I thought I would never do. I called my mother and told her that Ariel and I were coming to stay with her until I was able to find my own place. As much as I didn't want to live in Virginia, I knew that I had to get as far away from all the motherfuckers that wanted my head on a platter.

The next morning, I went to the car dealership and paid cash for a new car. I got my keys, set the GPS, and hit the road. The trip was about seven hours, depending on traffic. I turned on the radio to keep me company for the drive. I can honestly say that I felt like my life was finally going to go in the direction that I needed it to go. I thought about all that I risked for motherfuckers that didn't care for me and how stupid I was. All that mattered now was Ariel and my mom; they were all I needed. At least I didn't have to question if they loved me unconditionally.

When I called my mom, I had a long talk with her before deciding that Virginia would be my destination. She said that she never knew anything concerning Que and Toni, and I believed her. All the years that I secretly hated my mother, instead of just talking to her, hurt me. Me being bent on believing that everyone betrayed me caused her to miss out on the birth of her granddaughter. I just hoped that we could move forward and make up for lost time.

I was finally pulling up in my mother's driveway. The house looked different from the last time I was here which was when my grandmother passed away. It was about 10:00 pm, and I was tired and just wanted to sleep. My mom came out to help me with my bags, but I made sure to hold on to the suitcase that held the two duffel bags; I wasn't about to let that bag out of my sight. It had nothing to do with me not trusting my mom; it was just that my future was in those bags, so I wasn't taking any chances by letting them out of my sight.

I watched as a tall, slim, nice looking gentleman exited the house to assist my mom, and my face showed my disapproval. My mom never told me that she had a man living here with her. She saw my facial expression change, and she smiled nervously because she knew that I had always been an outspoken child, and I guess she didn't want me to ask who the fuck that nigga was. I stayed calm and decided to wait for her to tell me what was up with his ass. Had I not been so tired, I probably would have put that ass on blast. She showed me to the room that I would be staying in with Ariel. I wanted to tell her again that my staying with her was temporary, just until I found a place of my own, because with the way that she had it set up with a crib for Ariel, diapers, and a lot of other shit, she must have forgotten. Once I put my things down, I hugged my mom as she told me how much she missed me. She didn't make a big fuss over Ariel because she was sleeping; she just expressed how beautiful she was.

The next morning, I felt relaxed and refreshed as I went downstairs to fix something to eat. Entering the kitchen, I saw that my mom was already fixing breakfast. I had almost forgotten that I was at home with my mom again until I saw her standing in the kitchen.

"Good morning, Mom," I said, kissing her on the cheek.

"Morning, baby," she said, hugging me.

"Okay, so how did you forget to tell me that you had a man?" I asked her.

"I didn't forget to tell you I had a man; I just didn't feel that telling you over the phone was a good idea," she said.

"Mom, it would have been better for you to tell me over the phone than to have me come home, and he's here," I whined.

"Well, I didn't think it was a big deal enough deal to tell you on the phone, and I didn't expect him to be here when you arrived," she said.

"So, he doesn't live here?" I asked with raised eyebrows.

"No, he doesn't live here. We've only been seeing each other for a few months," she answered.

"How did you meet him?" I asked, prying.

"Wow, aren't we miss nosey this morning. I met him when I went to New York with your Aunt Trina for the weekend. Your aunt treated me to Applebee's; he was there with a couple of friends. He kept flirting with me with his eyes, and you already know how bold your aunt is, so she started talking to him about how we were grown women, and if he had something to say to me, he needed to do it like a gentleman. He asked if he could join us, and we agreed. He and I talked, and we found out that we both lived in Richmond. He was in New York for a family gathering, so we exchanged numbers. Once we got back to Richmond, he called me up. We went on a date and have been dating since," she explained, smiling.

"So you were in New York?" I asked.

"Yes, I was in New York, and had I knew where you were staying, trust, I would have came there with a strap. Don't you ever call yourself not speaking to me for all these years based on something you assumed," she joked, but I could see the hurt in her eyes.

"I'm sorry, Mom. I was in my feelings about what happened, and it clouded my judgment and my decision making," I said, giving her a hug. "So, tell me about this man of yours," I requested, breaking the hug.

"His name is Shaun. He's forty, and he has two twin daughters who he is in the process of trying to get custody of. He lives and works here in Richmond," she said, smiling from ear to ear.

"Do you love him?" I asked.

"It's only been a few months, so I wouldn't say that I love him, but I do like him a lot," she said.

"Okay, Stella. Get your groove back," I laughed before I had to run up the stairs to a crying Ariel.

My mom left the house later on that evening because she had a date with her new man, so it was just Ariel and I. She was sleeping, and I was looking online for a place of my own. Toni had been blowing my phone up, so I took it that he was back and had realized that he was broke. Didn't that nigga know that what goes around comes right back around?

If he didn't, he knows now. I was making it my business to get another phone tomorrow. Shit, it seems as if I've been changing phones like I change my damn underwear lately. Well, that's the price you pay when you're dodging motherfuckers left and right.

Chapter Thirty (Tasha)

We just got our lives back on point, and I must say that we are in a good place. We haven't had any problems from Jasmine in months, but for some reason, being stress free just isn't in the cards for me. I got a certified letter from a man claiming to be the father of the twins. Now when my sister passed away, I tried to find the twins' father to no avail. Now, after all of this time, he has a conscious, and he wants to be in his childrens' lives. Bullshit. So now, next month I have to go and take the twins to have a DNA test done so that when we go to the court date, paternity would be established already. I just couldn't catch a fucking break, and I swear my breaking point is near. I can just feel it.

Tonight, we were hanging out with Lah, Chink, Liem, and Polo at the Barclay's Center for a Nets game. It's not my cup of tea, but I was trying to be a good wife and do some of the things that my husband enjoyed doing. Polo and Chink weren't too happy about going to a basketball game either, but they agreed to do their wifey duties as well and that was keeping the husbands happy.

I'm not going to lie; we had a good time. After the game, we went out for drinks, and we had fun and really enjoyed each other company. Rellz and I have really been getting along, and he has been so attentive and showing public affection, making me feel good inside. I couldn't wait until we got home because I have not been giving up the pussy, but tonight, he earned it. He made me feel like I was the only woman in the world, and that meant so much to me. I'm not saying that all was forgotten, but I would say that I'm ready to stop being a prude about the whole situation because he has proven that home is where he wants to be.

"You two need to get a room," Polo said, laughing.

"We have a room, and I can't wait until we get there because I'm going to tear that pussy up," Rellz said.

"Rellz!" I shouted, punching him in his arm. He definitely had too much to drink.

"I think it's time for the check," Lah stated, causing all of us to laugh.

We had a few more drinks before calling it a night. We agreed to at least try to have date night together at least twice a month. Rellz held my hand the entire ride home, stealing glances and smiling. It felt like we were falling in love all over again. I tried not to get my hopes up too high because after each fuck up, he always turned into the Rellz that I had met in the beginning, just to change once shit was good again.

When we got home, we wasted no time as we stripped out of our clothes and went at it. Rellz pushed me down on

212

the bed. He put my legs on his shoulder and went to dinner on my clit, acting like he didn't just finish eating. I arched my back and rocked my hips up and down, enjoying his wet, thick tongue that I missed so much.

"Oh my God. Ohhhhhh, Rellzzzz. It feels so gooooood," I moaned.

I don't know what the hell he was doing to my body with his tongue, but tears fell from my eyes as I cried out. I felt myself cumming as his lips clamped down on my pussy, and he continued to tongue fuck me until my juices released in his mouth. Rellz didn't miss a beat as he kept me in the same position, entering me and fucking me like it had been years since he had any pussy. He took beating up the pussy to a new level as I screamed out from the pain and pleasure he was causing. His ass was on ten as he stood, lifting me with him. He now had me riding his dick as I grabbed him around his neck, making sure that he didn't drop my ass. Grabbing him around his neck also gave me leverage for a better ride on his dick.

I could tell that he was about to cum because his legs were getting weak. He laid me down on the bed and continued to beat up the pussy until we both came together. We lay still, breathing heavily. I turned on my side, and he pulled me to him, wrapping his arms around me and whispering in my ear that he loved me before I heard him snoring. I laid awake, silently crying, because of how much I loved this man, and I wondered if I was making the same mistake that I had made time and time again.

It hurt me that I didn't know if this time would be the real deal. I promise you that I wanted to believe in my husband, but it was hard. Here he just fucked the shit out me, and left me basking in the aftermath of great sex, but in the back of my head, I'm lying here wondering if he fucked her like he just fucked me. I didn't want to think of another woman that he fucked, but I just couldn't help it. I hoped that I could eventually get over it and just enjoy my husband again.

~

Rellz offered to go and pick the kids up from my aunt's house, so I was on my way to have lunch with Chink in the village. I got to Mighty Quinn's and stood out front to wait on her. Even though I was feigning for their barbeque, I was more interested in getting some advice from her. I was definitely conflicted, and I needed someone who had gone through the exact same situation. That someone was Chink.

"Hey, girl." I hugged her as she walked up.

"What's up?" she asked as we walked inside.

"I asked you to meet me for lunch because I'm conflicted and needed to talk to someone," I said, sighing.

"What's going on?" she asked.

"I don't want to bring up shit that happened months ago, but I'm feeling conflicted lately about forgiving Rellz. Don't get me wrong; he has been nothing short of the man that I met all of those years ago, but I just can't get him cheating with Jasmine out of my head. Last night was our first night being intimate since he came clean about all the shit that went down with her, and it was great, but as soon as it was over, I couldn't help but wonder if he fucked her the same way he had just fucked me," I said, being honest.

"Trust me when I say that I understand exactly where you're coming from and what you're going through. Lah was my first everything, and he had never cheated on me; this was a first for me, so when I found out that not only was he cheating but that he looked me in my face and lied, I was crushed. Me deciding to forgive him was mostly based on the fact that he had never cheated on me before, so he got a pass for that reason and that reason only. Now you have expressed that this isn't Rellz's first time cheating on you; in fact, you said you stopped counting. In my honest opinion, if Lah was Rellz, I wouldn't have been able to forgive him because I would have to ask myself when enough will be enough. Love tends to get us caught up and blind us to what we already know.

How many times have you asked yourself if he really means it this time and you convince yourself that the answer is yes, but deep down you already know that the answer to that question is no. Again, don't get me wrong; I'm not telling you to not stay with your husband, but if you stay and he does it again, you can't blame him. You have to blame yourself. I don't know if what I said makes any sense, but what I will say is that I like you, and I respect you as my friend, and I will support you with whatever you decide to do with your marriage. Now if Lah was to cheat on me again, he already knows not to come home because I will not be a fool, not even for the man that I love with my all," she finished, taking a sip of her drink.

I sat thinking about all that she said, and I could honestly respect that she was upfront and honest about it. I really didn't need anyone to tell me that I was playing the fool by taking him back, but I'm honestly not ready to give up on my husband just yet.

"Can I be honest with you?" she asked me.

"Yes, I wouldn't want it any other way," I said to her.

"When I first met your husband, he came on to me. Not in so many words, but I'm not going to lie; I was getting my flirt on too because I found him to be very attractive, but the difference between me and him was that I knew to not go any further than flirting. Rellz is a man, and he has a hard time resisting temptation, so I say this to you to explain that if I took the bait, not only would he have been sleeping with Jasmine, he would have been sleeping with me too," she said. I wasn't even mad because all she was trying to do was give me a reality check, and I respected her for it.

"Damn," I whispered because I didn't know what else to say.

I knew that she shared that piece of information to further help me with my decision, but again, it didn't deter me from wanting to be with my husband. I couldn't just follow my head on this one because my heart wasn't allowing me to forget how much I loved him.

Our food came, and I wasn't even hungry anymore as I pushed the plate from in front of me. I took a sip from my drink and sat in deep thought as she let me. I watched as she picked over her food.

"You seem like you have something on your mind too. Do you want to talk about it?" I asked her.

"I'm pregnant," she blurted out.

"Well, the baby isn't Rellz; is it?" I joked, causing her to spit out her drink, laughing.

"Sorry, I couldn't resist. You opened up the door for that one," I laughed. "Seriously, though. That's good news, so why do you seem so down about it?" I asked her.

"I don't know. I just feel like we just got back in a good place, and not to mention, I hardly have time for my shop as it is. Right now, I'm working part-time, and when this baby comes, I'm not going to be at the shop at all. It just feels like my dream is slipping away from me," she said.

"Don't look at it like that. It's your dream, so it will always be there. This pregnancy is a blessing, and you should be celebrating," I told her.

"I haven't even told Lah or Polo yet," she confided.

"Well, I'm not going to say anything but tell your husband that he's going to be a daddy again, and you better tell Polo that she's going to be a aunty again," I said.

"I know. He's been looking at me sideways since the night we went out because I didn't have a drink that night. He knows something is up; he just doesn't know what it is. I'm going to tell him; I just haven't decided if I want to have another child right now," she said.

"I didn't even think anything of you not wanting to drink that night. See how slow your girl is?" I laughed.

"Polo knows because she knows me better than I know myself, but she's waiting on me to tell her," she said.

"Well, you need to get to telling and have this conversation with your husband. Tell him exactly how you feel about having another child. You know he's not going to try and hear you about not wanting to have this baby, so I already know that we will be planning a baby shower," I said.

"Ugh. Decisions, decision," she said.

It was getting late. I had really enjoyed my time out with her, and I appreciated her listening to me and the advice that she had given me. I gave her a kiss on the cheek, thanking her as we said our goodbyes. When I got back to the house, the kids and Rellz were in the living room; he was playing cards with the twins. I walked over and greeted them with a kiss and a hello, and he told me that RJ and Madison were sleeping. I told him that I was going to go up and take a shower and that when the twins were down, I needed to talk to him.

I took a long, hot shower to try and ease some of the stress I'd been feeling lately. Did it work? Nope, but it didn't stop me from putting my big girl panties on to have this talk with my husband. When I got to the bedroom, he was already sitting on the edge of the bed. He was in defensive mode, waiting on me, and I chickened out. I went to my top drawer and pulled out the certified envelope that came the other day and handed it to him. I watched as he looked it over; I knew he was upset because his forehead showed the stress lines, and his jaw was tightening. I was getting nervous because he hadn't said anything yet.

"Is this a fucking joke?" he asked, a few minutes later.

"No, it came in the mail the other day," I said.

"So why the fuck are you just showing me this shit now?" he barked.

"I was going to tell you; I just wanted to make sure the shit was legit and if we had to oblige. Once I found out that it was legit and we had to get the test done and appear to court on the date that's on the paper, I knew it was time to tell you," I said nervously.

"Where has this nigga been all this fucking time? We looked for his bitch ass and left messages for his ass, and he never showed. So, why now?" he asked, throwing the papers on the floor and walking out of the room.

I knew that he was going to be upset because the twins were his. He took to them from the day that they came to live with us, so I knew how he felt about a stranger trying to take them from us. Yes, he may be their biological father, but he's still a stranger. I went downstairs to make sure that he was okay. I was praying that by the time the court date came, Turk would be back in town because I needed him to keep

Rellz from hurting the man that was taking us to court. I found him sitting in the dark, with the only light coming from the moonlight outside of the window.

"Tash, I'm not about to sit back and agree to let some fucking man that they don't know, a fucking stranger, take them from us," he said.

I just went and sat next to him on the couch, with him holding me. I silently prayed again that Turk got his ass back here. His daughter lives with her mother in Canada, and he always goes to visit her twice a month, but this is the longest he's ever stayed gone. I could have called Kane, but Kane wasn't going to be able to stop him from killing anybody. If anything, Kane probably wouldn't see anything wrong with it because he's going to feel the same way Rellz does.

Chapter Thirty-One (Chink)

I finally told Lah about me being pregnant and he was so happy, but in the back of my head, I was still having doubts. It's not that I wouldn't love to have my little girl or another little boy, but I just feel the timing isn't right. He got a little upset when he saw that I wasn't as happy as he was, but I tried to explain to him that we were still working on getting our relationship where it used to be, and I just felt that a baby would complicate it more - kind of how some couples mistake sex for love. I didn't want him to think that just because we were having another baby that all that we discussed about me taking forgiving him and learning to trust him again slow would change. I love him and I do feel like we are almost back to how our relationship has always been, but I still have my doubts. I was in the kitchen, making breakfast, before it was time for us to go to my first doctor's appointment. I swear I was trying to be happy, but for some reason, it just wasn't happening.

Lah pulled up to North Shore Hospital for my first appointment at the OB/GYN clinic. Lah and LJ went to sit in the waiting area while I let the receptionist know that I was here. I sat down to fill out all of the annoying paperwork that I really wasn't in the mood to fill out; it was asking all those questions that the doctor was going to end up asking again anyway. I handed the clipboard back to the receptionist and went back to sit down. LJ was busy messing with just about every magazine on the table.

"Are you okay, babe?" Lah asked me.

"I'm okay," I said, being short with him.

"Well, it doesn't seem like you're okay to me. You have been wearing a mean mug ever since you got up this morning," he said, causing me to get defensive.

"I'm not wearing a mean mug, and for your information, I'm just tired," I replied, rolling my eyes.

"Whatever. I'm not going to keep kissing your ass. If you don't want to have the fucking baby then don't have it," he said, embarrassing me in front of all of the other people in the waiting area.

I couldn't believe that he had just done that as I watched him and LJ walk out to the elevator. I was so embarrassed and wished that I could just disappear. I was too happy when the nurse called my name to go to the back. I gave her the wait signal while I went to see if Lah and LJ were standing in the hallway near the elevators, but of course, they weren't. I tried to hold in the tears that were threatening to fall, but one escaped.

"Are you okay?" the nurse asked me.

"I'm fine," I lied, following her to the room that she was placing me in.

Thirty minutes later, I was done with my appointment. I was now waiting for my prescription and the date for my next appointment. I thought that Lah would cool off and come back upstairs, but he didn't. I was surprised to see that he didn't leave my ass because he was still parked in the same spot. As I got closer to the car, I noticed that he wasn't in the car, so I picked up my phone to call him.

"Where are you?" I asked when he answered the phone.

"Are you done?" he asked.

All I got out was yes before he ended the call. I wanted to tell him that I was already at the car, but he didn't give me the chance to finish. I knew that he was upset, but he was doing too much, leaving my first doctor's appointment was real childish on his part. I watched as him and LJ came walking from the other side of the street. He unlocked the door, and I got inside, not saying another word to him. If he wanted to act childish, I could act childish too. LJ was too busy playing with the toy that his father bought him to even notice that Mommy and Daddy were mad at each other.

Lah drove the rest of the way home, not speaking to me, and that was fine because I didn't have anything to say to his ass. I didn't even tell him that I needed to go by the pharmacy to put my prescription in because I figured I would get to the house, get my car, and do it my damn self. When he pulled up to the house, I got out of the car, pulled my car keys out of my bag, hopped in my car, and pulled off. I wasn't about to do this with Lah; I already had a lot on my mind, and I didn't need his ass adding to it. Not even a minute later, my phone was alerting me that I had a text message. I waited until I got to the CVS parking lot before looking at the text message.

Lah: So that's how we're doing it now? You just hop in your car and pull out?

Me: Did you not just do the same damn thing, leaving my appointment?

Lah: Why should I stay at your appointment when you don't even want my fucking baby?

Me: Who said that I didn't want to have your baby, Lah?

Lah: You didn't have to say it. Your attitude had said it all since the day you told me about the damn pregnancy.

Me: Well, my attitude has nothing to do with me being pregnant, Lah, and had you just been patient, you would have known why I was feeling the way I'm feeling.

Lah: How many times do I have to ask you what's wrong for you to keep telling me nothing? Clearly something is wrong, so no, I couldn't be patient. We're grown, and by you shutting me out, all it did was piss me off.

Me: Lah, I'm about to go into the pharmacy, so I will see you as soon as I get my prescription filled.

I wasn't about to keep going back and forth with his ass, especially when he was acting the same age as his fucking son. I paid for my prescription, grabbed a bag of sunflower seeds, and kept it moving. No, I wasn't in any rush to get back home, but I didn't want to be out here either. I called Polo up because she was the only one who could get me out of my funk, but she was giving Paris a bath, so she said that she would call me back. When I got back to the house, Lah was sitting on the couch. He was wearing the mean mug now, but I didn't even let it faze me.

"So, why do you feel the need to act childish, Lah?" I asked him.

"I wasn't acting childish, but tell me how the fuck do you expect me to act when you're walking around, acting like you don't want to have my fucking seed," he barked.

"Like I asked you earlier, who said that I didn't want your baby? All I expressed was that I didn't think that now was a good time; that's all."

"That's the same shit as not wanting my fucking baby, Chink," he said, continuing to be loud.

"Look, I'm not trying to argue with you about something that doesn't matter because I'm having the baby. I've just been down lately because I'm going to have another baby with no mom to share it with, so that's why I was really feeling more sad than happy about being pregnant again," I said, deciding to just tell him the truth.

"And why did you feel that you couldn't just tell me that, Chink? I know I fucked up and lost your trust, but you can always trust that you can talk to me and that I will be here for you," he said.

My crybaby ass was at it again because he always says some shit that touches me and has me all in my feelings. I know that he was tired of seeing me cry, but he would have to get used to it because now that I'm pregnant, I'm probably going to be in my feelings all the time.

"I apologize for leaving the appointment. What did the doctor say?" he asked me, wiping my tears.

"He said that I'm six weeks pregnant, he did a vaginal exam, asked a few questions, and gave me my prescription and my next appointment. That was it," I said.

"Cool. I hope that we get a little girl this time, but if it's a boy, I'm cool with that too," he said.

"Well, I'm hoping for a little girl so that she and Paris can be best friends like me and Polo," I smiled. Lah leaned over to kiss me before going to check on LJ. Just as he walked out of the room, my phone rang, and it was Polo. I quickly filled her in on what happened between Lah and me, and then she told me about the conversation that Liem had initiated with her.

Polo said that Liem approached her, having doubts about why Jared had snatched her. Polo said that she explained to him that Jared had fixated in his mind that they had a relationship and that she has left him for Liem. Jared felt that Polo should have been with him, and Paris should have been his child, and when she reminded him that they had never had a sexual relationship and were only friends, he started punching her.

Polo started to cry as she recounted to me how she kicked him when he tried to take her pants off, and after she ran, he caught her and continued to beat her until they heard the glass shatter. I held my breathe when she told me how Liem had asked her if Jared had violated her sexually, knowing that her and I had never had that conversation either, and I could hear the smile in her voice when she told me what her response to Liem had been. 'No, he didn't get the chance to because you came right on time, and I will always be thankful that you saved me.'

Just as Polo finished her story, I could hear Liem in the background as LJ and Lah rejoined me in the living room. Polo and I ended our conversation as Lah and LJ snuggled close to me on the couch. It was getting late, so we decided to order some pizza and wings because we were going to make it a movie night. Just me and my two favorite guys.

Chapter Thirty-Two (Tasha)

One Month Later

Today was the court date, and I was nervous as hell because the thought of the twins being taken from us was stressing me the hell out. I was praying that the DNA test results showed that he was not the father. Not to talk about my sister, but she was out there, and this was one time I was praying that she was sleeping around when she got pregnant with the twins. Rellz just sat on the edge of the bed, doing everything in slow motion. He had yet to put his clothes on; instead, he was on his phone. What he was doing, I didn't know, but I wished that he would make moves because I didn't want to be late.

"Rellz, I need for you to start getting dressed because we have to be there at 9:30, and it's already 9:00," I said.

"How about we don't show up and I wait for the faggot ass nigga to leave the courthouse and put some heat in his ass?" he asked, seriously.

"If he ends up dead, who do you think is the first person they are going to investigate?" I answered, just as serious.

"Tash, I don't give a fuck about all that bullshit. That nigga isn't about to get custody and take our fucking girls from us," he barked.

I decided to just leave it alone because I knew that he was feeling this way because Raina's grandmother took him to court after Rena was killed, and they have shared custody. Now that Rena's mom no longer lives in New York, he doesn't get to see Raina anymore when her grandmother has her. The judge fucked him in that custody battle, so he was probably feeling as if he was about to be fucked again.

We got to the courthouse on time; I didn't see the lawyer, so we decided to just go inside and wait. Inside the courtroom, my face lit up because Lah, Chink, Polo, and Liem were already there to show their support. Rellz and I sat down next to them to wait on the lawyer. My ass felt like I was about to have a panic attack; that's how nervous I was. I tried to calm myself down by listening to the case that was being discussed.

The courtroom door opened, and I turned around to see if it was the lawyer, but what I saw caused my fists to ball, and my breathing to increase. I couldn't believe that, after all this time, the bitch that I hated the most was only standing a few feet away from me, and I couldn't touch her. I guess Rellz felt my body tense up, so he turned in the direction that I was looking in, and it was like a domino effect as we were now all staring the bitch down. Rellz stood up, and I pulled him back down, letting him know that he couldn't do anything to her in the courtroom because, without a doubt, he would be locked up.

I was trying to figure out what the fuck the bitch was doing here in the first place. It didn't take long to get my answer once I saw the man, that I had only seen in pictures, come up from behind her with another woman. I watched as they sat down a few rows behind us on the opposite side. I started to wonder if this bitch was at it again. Was she the reason this man was now asking to be a part of the twins' lives? I noticed that Rellz was having a hard time sitting still because he wanted to get at the bitch about the whereabouts of his daughter.

I put my hand on his knee, trying to calm him down. I whispered in his ear that she wasn't going to leave without letting us know where his child was. She was going to be able to leave still breathing being we couldn't get at her like we wanted to, but she wasn't leaving without telling him where the fuck his daughter was because I would beat her ass first.

I saw him discreetly texting on his phone, so I already knew that he was on it, so that bitch would be dealt with soon. The lawyer for the twins walked in, and I rolled my eyes because I wasn't too pleased with him; I didn't understand why we had to wait until the court date to find out if this man, Shaun, was the twins' father or not. The judge called the case, and both lawyers approached with Shaun and me following as we sat on opposite sides of the table. I held my breath as the judge started to speak.

"These results were prepared by DNA Diagnostics, and they read as follows: In the case of Saniyah and Shaina Jenkins, it is so ordered that Shaun Smith is the father," she said.

"This is some fucking bullshit," Rellz yelled, leaving the courtroom.

When the judge said that she was granting temporary custody to this man, who is a fucking stranger to my nieces, I cried. I stood, defeated, as I walked out of the courtroom. This bitch, Jasmine, had the nerve to smirk at me on my way out, and it took everything in me not to snatch the bitch up. Rellz was sitting on the bench right outside of the courtroom. The lawyer came over and explained that we had to hand the girls over on Friday. He said that we were scheduled to come back to court in three weeks to schedule visitation. I had already made up my mind to hire a lawyer to fight for sole custody; this man was never a part of their lives, and they didn't know him, so for the judge to grant sole custody to him wasn't fair. If I even thought that the judge was going to grant him temporary custody, I would have gotten my own lawyer. Rellz tried to tell me that this bullshit was going to happen, but I didn't believe him because in Raina's grandmother's case, Raina was actually living with her before Rena passed, but the twins had never even met this man.

The courtroom door opened, and before I knew it, Rellz was up and in Shaun's face. I tried to stop him, but it was too late. I didn't need Rellz to fuck up our chances of even getting visitation by showing that he had a temper that he couldn't control. I expected Lah and Liem to intervene, but they stood at his side like they were ready to pop off too. Now wasn't the time for them to have his back; I needed for them to be the voice of reason before we lost our chances of even fighting for custody.

"Why now, nigga? Where the fuck you been all this time? We reached out to your family, and no fucking body was interested in taking the twins, so again, why the fuck now?" Rellz asked him.

"First off, you need to watch your tone. Second, you reaching out to my family has nothing to do with me. And as far as why now, have you ever heard the saying, better late than never, nigga?" he said, walking off.

"Rellz, noooo!" I screamed as I saw him lift his hand to hit Shaun.

It was too late as I watched Rellz hit Shaun in the back of the head, dazing him but not knocking him down. Shaun turned around, not backing down, as him and Rellz starting fighting. The lawyer ran inside of the courtroom, I guess to get some assistance. Had this been criminal court, he wouldn't have had to get help; they have officers all over the damn place. I begged Liem and Lah to break it up. I saw the woman that was with him look as if she was about to make a move. I didn't know if she was going to try and break it up, or if she was going to jump in, so I jumped on her ass. Jasmine ran up on me, just to get pulled back by Polo, who threw her ass across the floor like she was a rag doll.

Court officers rushed in from all directions, pulling all parties apart. I just knew that we all were about to be locked up. When the court officer asked us all to leave, he didn't have to ask us twice. I knew that the only reason we were walking out of here was because this was family court. Jasmine was still trying to pop off, talking about I attacked her mother. First off, I didn't know that it was her mother because I had never met her mother. To be honest, I didn't care if it was her grandmother. If the bitch jumped bad and went after my man, she would have gotten the same treatment.

Rellz started yelling at her about where his fucking daughter was; I guess the court officers were getting fed up with the back and forth because they threatened that we would all be locked up if we didn't leave now. I wasn't about to be locked up, so I grabbed Rellz by his arm and escorted him out of the building. Once outside, on the courtroom steps, I was witnessing a scene out of a movie as I heard tires screeching as two vans came to a stop. I already knew what time it was, but it was too late as gunshots rang out. Everyone that was outside was trying not to get caught in the crossfire. All I heard was screams, as I stood frozen before being thrown to the ground by Rellz.

The gunshots stopped as quickly as they started, and once I heard the screeching of the tires again, I knew that the vans' gunmen were fleeing the scene. I tried to get up, but Rellz's body weight didn't allow me to. Panic started to set in as I feared the worst when he didn't respond to me telling him to get up. Sirens blared out as the emergency units were now on the scene. Rellz was lifted up off of me, and I screamed out to him as they worked on him. There was so much going on that I didn't even see Polo, Chink, or Lah. I desperately wanted to know if they were okay, but I couldn't go and look for them as I got into the ambulance to ride to the hospital with Rellz.

Chapter Thirty-Three (Chink)

I didn't know what the fuck was going on, but as we were about to leave out of the courthouse, shots rung out. Rellz and Tasha had already exited, and I was trying to go out to see if they were okay, but the officers weren't allowing anyone to leave. I prayed that they were okay because there was a lot of screaming and people banging on the door to be let back in, but the officers weren't allowing anyone back into the building either. It seemed like forever before they allowed us to leave. Once outside, blood stained the steps of the courthouse, but Tasha and Rellz weren't outside. I approached one of the officers and was told that a few people were rushed to the hospital, so that was where we were headed. I tried not to fear the worst, but my gut was telling me that one, or both, of them were hurt. Lah was driving mad slow, and I wanted to tell him to put the pedal to the medal, but I didn't.

Once at the hospital, we asked if they had a Rellz or Tasha Jackson, and they directed us to the emergency room area. As soon as we walked in the emergency room area, there was chaos as family members were in there trying to inquire about their loved ones. I heard the security guard say that twenty people were bought in with gunshot wounds, and I started to cry. He advised all of the families to have a seat and said that someone would be out with information on all of the victims soon. That shit didn't work for me; I needed to know if they were okay because I wasn't strong enough to play the waiting game without losing it.

Lah told me that I needed to calm down and remember that I was pregnant and didn't need to stress myself, but how could I not stress that my friend and her husband may be dead? Polo held my hand as we sat down and waited for someone to come out and tell us something. About ten minutes later, a nurse came out and called for the family members of the victims. We waited but the family of Rellz and Tasha Jackson weren't called. The families followed the nurse, and panic tried to seep in, but I closed my eyes and calmed myself. When one of the family members, that had just went into the back, came out screaming and crying, Polo and I automatically started to cry; it was hard not to because we felt the woman's pain as she screamed for her child. Just as Lah was going to say something to me, I saw Tasha walk out from the back, and I jumped up with them all following behind me

"OMG! Tasha, I thought you were dead," I cried out, hugging her.

"I'm fine; Rellz was shot," she cried.

"Is he okay? What are they saying?" Lah asked her.

"He was rushed into surgery; he was shot in the leg and back. When he threw me to the ground, he hit his head. He was unconscious when the emergency unit got there, but they told me that when he went in for surgery, he was conscious and knew that he was shot," she said.

"So is there a waiting area that we can wait in for him to come out of surgery?" I asked her.

"Yeah, I couldn't get a signal in the back, so I came out to give you guys a call and to call his parents to let them know what was going on. Jasmine is here also. She was shot, but I don't know how serious her injuries are," she said, looking sad.

I wanted to say that I didn't give a fuck about that bitch being shot, but instead, I actually felt sorry for her and found myself praying that she was okay. Something about watching that mother cry for her dead child did something to me and had me not wanting to wish death on anyone, even if it was Jasmine. After Tasha made her calls, we went to the back to wait for Rellz to come out of surgery. When we got to the back, there were a lot of people there waiting as well, including the woman who we now knew was Jasmine's mother. My heart broke as she sat in the corner alone, crying for her child.

"Do you think we should say something to Jasmine's mother? I feel so sorry for her right now," I asked them.

"I don't think you should approach her right now. Tasha just jumped on her, so I doubt if she's going to want to talk to any of us," Lah said, and I agreed.

Rellz was out of surgery and now in recovery. We didn't think that he would be in surgery so long. It was getting late, so I doubted if we were going to see him tonight. Even if they did allow visitors tonight, his father and mother were here, so we decided that we were going to go because as long as he was okay, we could see him tomorrow. We all took turns giving Tasha a hug before leaving the hospital. I was mentally and physically tired; I just wanted to get off of this emotional ride that I was on. I had gone through so much in my life, and it was getting harder and harder to stay above water. I honestly feel like I'm losing control. I feel like I haven't fully recovered from losing my mom and Karen, and now this added stress of Lah being unfaithful and almost losing Rellz is pushing me over the top.

"Babe, you okay?" Lah asked me.

"I just don't know how much more stress I can handle before I have a breakdown," I answered honestly.

"I can't say that I know how you're feeling and what you're going through because you have been through a lot. It hurts me that I have added to what you were already dealing with, but I promise you that I'm here, and I will never let you down again," he promised.

"Lah, we're good. If I didn't believe that you weren't going to hurt me again, I would have never forgiven you. I'm just feeling some kind of way about all that has happened and is continuing to happen," I said.

We talked up until he pulled up to the house. All I wanted to do was shower and get into the bed because my ass was tired. Lah said that he wanted to call Tasha to check on Rellz one more time before he called it a night. When I got out of the shower, he said that Rellz was moved to a room, and his mother stayed with him so that Tasha could go home, get out of those clothes, shower, and get some rest before coming back to the hospital tomorrow. As soon as my head hit the pillow, I felt my eyes get heavy, and in a matter of minutes, I was out.

Chapter Thirty-Four (Tasha)

I had just gotten out of the shower, and as soon as I was about to get in the bed, I heard someone knocking at the door as the same time that my phone was ringing. I answered my phone, and it was Turk, telling me to unlock the door. *'What the hell is he doing here at three in the morning,'* I thought as I put on my robe to let him in.

"Turk, what are you doing here? I thought you said that you were going to fly in tomorrow?" I asked him.

"I know, but I couldn't wait until tomorrow. I needed to get back to make sure that he was good. I went to the hospital, but I wasn't able to see him, so I came here," he said.

"He's out of recovery and in a room, so visiting hours aren't until tomorrow at 12. Had you called me, I would have told you that."

"I wasn't thinking. When you called me, I knew that I wasn't going to wait until tomorrow to leave. What the fuck happened?" he asked me.

"I know how you feel because I didn't want to leave the hospital tonight, but his mother insisted that I come home and get some rest."

"So are you going to tell me what happened, or do I have to read about it in the newspaper?" he asked, smiling.

"Well, you have been gone so long this time, so Rellz didn't get a chance to tell you all the shit that has been going on. Anyway, I don't know if you knew but Rellz was sleeping with Jasmine, and her daughter belongs to him. The twins' father filed for custody of them, so we had to take the twins to have a DNA test done to establish paternity. Yesterday was the court date; shit didn't go good at all. It turns out that he is their father, and the judge granted him temporary custody. Rellz stormed out of the courtroom, and when the twins' father exited the courtroom, Rellz approached him. They started fighting, all hell broke loose, and we were all asked to leave. Once outside, two black vans came out of nowhere and started shooting. Rellz got hit, and so did Jasmine." I didn't even realize that I was crying. I had tried to be so strong throughout everything that had been going on, but it was starting to be too much.

"Damn, Tasha. I'm so sorry that this happened to you. I had no idea that he was sleeping with Jasmine; that shit was on the low for real. I'm not saying that if I had known, I would have said anything, but I promise you that I didn't know. Now about what happened at the courthouse. Did you see anything that would give me an idea as to who those niggas were?"

"It happened so fast that I didn't get a chance to see any of the gunmen's' faces. Rellz knocked me to the ground, so the whole time the shooting was going on, he was lying on top of me. I was so scared, and then when the shooting stopped, I tried to get up but I couldn't. I told Rellz to get up off of me, and he didn't move. At the time, I thought he was dead," I continued to cry.

"Tasha, don't cry. He's okay now, and I'm sorry that I wasn't here for all that you guys were going through. I wish I could take away all that you're feeling right now because you know I don't like to see you hurting," he said, taking me into his arms.

I closed my eyes, trying to block out the feelings that I once had for this man, but being in his arms, with just a robe on, wasn't helping. I know that my man was lying up in the hospital, and I shouldn't be thinking about the next man, but to be feeling some type of way about why Rellz always cheated on me had me feeling like something was wrong with me. So, to have this man here, who has always told me how much he loved me and that he would never hurt me, was clouding my judgment right now. I just wanted him to make me feel wanted. I know that I was wrong for the way that I was feeling, but this was something that I need right now as I reached up and kissed him on his lips.

"Tasha, what are you doing?" he asked.

"I'm sorry," I said, feeling rejected.

"Look, Tasha. You know how I feel about you because I have told you, but this isn't right. You chose Rellz, and I fell back because I respected your decision. I understand that you're feeling vulnerable right now, but I can't do this to myself again," he said. I understood fully, but I needed him right now. I needed to feel loved by someone that I knew loved me without question, and that just happened to be him.

"I'm not trying to put you in a fucked up situation again, but I need you right now. I just need to feel loved," I begged.

He didn't say anything; he just looked at me. I moved closer to him, kissing him on his lips again and apologizing between each kiss until he gave in, kissing me back. I let the robe fall to the floor as I straddled him, right there on the couch that I spent many nights on having movie night with my husband. Turk hungrily caressed my body as he pushed his tongue into my mouth, kissing me with so much passion that I felt the love. We made love all morning, and he did things to my body that made me cry out for him. I didn't want it to end; I wanted to stay in his arms for as long as I could, but I knew that I needed to get to the hospital to see about my husband. I was in love with my husband, but I couldn't deny that I loved Turk. As much as I tried to ignore it and even deny it, the fact still remained that the heart never lies.

Chapter Thirty-Five (Jasmine)

I have never been so scared in my life as when I heard those gunshots ring out. My mother and Shaun knew to get down on the ground, but by the time my brain told my legs to move so that I could get down, I was hit with a barrage of bullets. One of them severed my spinal cord, leaving me paralyzed. My whole world shattered when the doctors told me that I would never walk again. Can you imagine being fully independent, and then, all of a sudden, you're paralyzed? I can't care for my child the way that I needed too; I can't care for my bodily functions, and it really hurt me to my core. Everyday tasks are beyond challenging, and I just want to give up on most days.

The money that I stole from Toni is almost gone because most of it has been used for my medical bills. I still live with my mom, and she does as much as she can to help me, but it has become too much for her, taking care of my child and me. I have a full-time home health aide now, and my self-esteem is at an all-time low. Tasha has reached out, telling me how sorry she was about what happened to me, and I honestly believe her. She also asked if Rellz could have visitation on the same schedule that Shaun has when he visits the twins. I told her that I would think about it. I wanted to run it by my mom because I was thinking about giving Ariel to her father because I couldn't care for her anymore. I do believe that I'm being punished for all of the wrong doings that I've done, and all of the people that I hurt, so I have no choice but to accept my punishment, even though I feel like I would have been better off losing my life because this life that I now live is torture.

I heard that because Toni no longer had the money that he stole from Que, he had to move back home to live with his brother. The information of him being back at home got back to Que, and his brother's house was set on fire, with both of them inside. Now don't quote me on that, because it was rumored that Que was responsible, but when I saw it on the news, it was being ruled accidental. I feel bad that he lost his life, but he had to know that he wouldn't be able to rob someone like Que for that kind of money and walk away without being touched.

Chapter Thirty-Six (Chink)

I was now four months pregnant, and things have seemed to get back to how they were before Jasmine turned our worlds upside down. The shootout at the courthouse had nothing to do with any of us; some well-established man, who was being taken to court for child support, figured that if he had his child and her mother killed, he wouldn't have to pay. That was the same woman who was at the hospital, crying out for her child. I just didn't understand his logic; so you no longer have to pay child support, but you will be locked up for the rest of your life.

Rellz made a full recovery, thank God. Jasmine wasn't so lucky; she will never walk again, and although I believe that karma is a bitch and one might say that she got what she deserved, in my heart, I forgave her and felt sorry that she had to spend the rest of her life in a wheelchair. Rellz has tried to reach out to her for visitation with his daughter, but she still hasn't responded to any of his attempts. His and Tasha's marriage has been strained, and I think I know the reason why, but she's not saying. I believe that she has finally gotten fed up, but if my assumptions are right, I honestly believe that she's going about it the wrong way.

The twins were with Shaun for about three days before he brought them back to New York. They cried every day because they didn't know him. He agreed to work out an agreement where he stayed in New York and had supervised visits with them until they felt comfortable enough to at least have visits with him without Tasha or Rellz being present. It's been a few months, and they still didn't feel comfortable with him. I honestly don't believe that they ever will. He's a stranger, and they acknowledges Rellz as their father, so no matter how many talks Tasha has had with them about trying to get to know Shaun, they are not trying to hear it.

Lah, LJ, and I were on our way to my doctor's appointment. Today we would be finding out the sex of our little bun in the oven, and I was so excited. We pulled up to the hospital to a smiling Tasha and Polo standing outside, waiting on us. We have a bond with Tasha that would make you believe that Polo and I have known her for just as long as we have known each other. I got out of the car, hugging them and thanking them for coming.

"Did you think that I was going to miss this appointment? I want to know if you're having a little princess or another big head little boy," Polo said, laughing.

"I'm having a little princess; I just know it, but if it's another big head little boy, I'm going to be happy too. As long as my little one is healthy, I'm good, but I do want a little girl," I added as I laughed.

"Well, let's get inside, so the guessing game can be over, and we will know for sure," Lah said, rushing us inside.

"Just know that if it's a little girl, I will not be leaving with you because my girls and I are going shopping for my little diva," I said, walking inside.

It was confirmed that I was having another big head little boy. I was a little disappointed but still happy all the same. I still ended up leaving with Polo and Tasha so that we could go and get something to eat and catch up since we haven't been out in a while. We ended up going to the Outback that was located in the mall.

"So what's been going on with you lately, Tasha?" I asked her because I have been waiting to get the tea for a minute now.

"What do you mean what's going on with me?" She answered my question with a question, clearly stalling.

"I want to know what's going on with you and Turk," I said.

"Is it that obvious that's something is going on?" she asked.

"It's not; I'm just very observant, and I noticed that whenever Rellz is showing you any type of affection and Turk is present, he excuses himself," I said.

"Turk and I have a story; a story that I really would need a couple of days to share, so I will save that for another time. Anyway, the short version is that I have been harboring feelings for him for a very long time, and the night that he came to the house when Rellz got shot, I seduced him, and we slept together. We haven't slept together since that night, but we have been doing a lot of low key flirting and talking and texting whenever Rellz isn't home," she said.

"I'm not one to judge, but I would suggest that if you don't want to be with Rellz anymore then you should tell him because if not, it's just going to be a Jasmine situation all over again. And I'm telling you right now, I'm not about to go through that shit again with Rellz trying to kill our asses," Polo laughed.

"Trust me when I say that I love both men, but I'm in love with my husband. It just feels good to get the attention that I crave from Turk. The night that he came over to the house, I needed him to fill that void that I was feeling at the time, and he served that purpose, nothing more. I will always have love for him, but it will not go any further than what it is right now," she said, not knowing that she was playing a dangerous game.

We enjoyed our lunch, leaving the conversation about Turk alone, with me hoping that Rellz didn't end up killing both of their asses. Tasha admitted that she reached out to Jasmine through Shaun to try and get her to allow Ariel to visit when Shaun came up to visit with the girls. Jasmine has yet to send her, but she did say that she would think about it. She also admitted that she felt bad about what happened to Jasmine, and I told her that I felt the same way. Polo was like, "Fuck that bitch; she got what she deserved," causing Tasha to spill her drink, laughing.

It wasn't funny, but the way she just blurted it out made it funny. We finished lunch and headed out. We said our goodbyes to Tasha, telling her we would talk to her later. Polo and I did some shopping at the Children's Place, overdoing it for LJ, Paris, and the new baby. We hadn't really been spending any alone time with each other since we became friends with Tasha, and it felt good with just the two of us hanging out. We laughed and joked like we used to do as teenagers. I hated that our day together came to an end as she dropped me off at home, promising to call me when she got home.

Chapter Thirty-Seven (Chink)

Six months later

"Chink, push. Come on, baby. One more big push," Lah coached.

"I can't. It hurts too much," I cried, pushing his hand away from me.

"Come on, Chink. You've got this, girl. One more big push so I can meet my nephew," Polo cheered me on.

"Ugh; if you want to meet him, then you push him out," I yelled.

I felt like closing my legs and getting in the fetal position. My ass listened to Lah about doing it naturally, and now my ass was paying for it because the pain was too much to bare. They keep saying one more push, but the doctor said that the last one would be the one more push, and I was tired of pushing. Lah held my hand as he begged me to push one more time.

"Okay, Mrs. Morales. This is it. Push. One more big push. I see the head; he's almost out," the doctor said, sounding all excited like this was his first delivery.

I pushed as hard as I could, and my baby boy was born. I laid back, exhausted but happy that he was finally out. Lah cut the cord, and the nurse laid the baby on my chest. I was tired, and Polo was getting on my nerves with that damn camera in my face. As soon as the nurse removed the baby, I closed my eyes and drifted off to sleep. When I woke up, I was already out of recovery and was now in a private room. Lah was sitting in the chair, feeding the baby that we have yet to name. LJ was sleeping at the foot of my bed; he must have been exhausted too because I was in labor for like six hours.

"Hey, sleepy head. You were out for like three hours. I had to keep checking to see if you were still breathing," Lah laughed.

"I was tired. This delivery wore me out; I should have gotten an epidural because the pain was excruciating. Let me see my little man; you know we have to name him," I said.

"I know. Everybody was asking me what his name was, and I had to tell them that we had to wait until you woke up. You had so many visitors, but they all saw how tired you were, so they will be back tomorrow. Mama D said he looks just like me, but I think he looks like you," he smiled.

I held him in my arms and fell in love. He was so handsome, and I have to agree with Lah; he does favor me. He has my skin tone, nose, and the same chink to his eyes - just like mine.

"How do you like Lahmell James Morales?" I asked him.

"I love it, but we can't call him LJ," he laughed, causing me to laugh with him.

"Well I guess we have to call him Lil Lah or Mell," I said.

"Let's just call him Baby Lah for now," he said, kissing him on the forehead.

Over the next two days, I had so many visitors from Lah's father's side of the family. They all came bearing gifts that we didn't need any more of because we got so much stuff at my baby shower that I didn't have room in the nursery for any more stuff. I was being released today from the hospital, so Lah and I were just completing the paternity papers. We attempted to do them yesterday, but I wasn't feeling well, so he had to tend to the baby. I was feeling much better today, and I couldn't wait to get home and continue our journey with our newest member of the family.

This has been a hell of a ride that Lah and I have been on, and I'm happy to say that we were able to get off the ride, still standing. I'm not going to say that it was an easy task to forgive him and to learn to trust him again, but I did it. I believe in my heart that we will forever be bonded by love.

The End

Made in the USA
Columbia, SC
02 July 2018